THE BILLIONAIRE'S VENGEANCE

BRI BLACKWOOD

BRETAGEY PRESS

First Digital Edition: June 2022

Cover Designed by Amanda Walker PA and Design

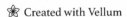 Created with Vellum

NOTE FROM THE AUTHOR

Hello!

Thank you for taking the time to read this book. The Billionaire's Possession is a dark billionaire enemies-to-lovers romance. It is not recommended for minors and contains situations that are dubious and could be triggering. The book also includes sexual assault and flashbacks to child abuse which might also be triggering.

It isn't a standalone and the book ends with a happily ever after. Make sure you read The Billionaire's Auction and The Billionaire's Possession before reading this book. This trilogy is complete.

BLURB

Taking him down in a ball of flames...

My world had come crashing down as I stared at her.

She laid before me, helpless, and I knew it was my fault.

Darkness settled upon me.

But it was soon followed by rage.

I'd been holding back, but there was no turning around now.

If he thought I wouldn't seek vengeance,

He'd better think again.

PLAYLIST

Start a War - Klergy, Valerie Broussard
Everybody Wants To Rule The World - Lorde
Immigrant Song - Remaster - Led Zeppelin
Sacrifice - Bebe Rexha
The Bitch Is Back - Elton John
Castle - Halsey
Holiday - Little Mix
A Little Wicked - Valerie Broussard
Hold My Hand - Lady Gaga

The playlist can be found on Spotify.

1

HARLOW

THE MORNING OF THE ACCIDENT

"I love you."

Although I'd just been woken up way too early in the morning, it was all worth it just to hear him say that. Would I ever get used to him saying those three simple but so meaningful little words? "And I love you too. Now, you have to get ready to head into the city for your board meeting."

"I'm tempted to call in and have the meeting rescheduled."

I snorted as I sat up in bed. "Do you realize how bad that would look?"

"Do you think I care? I want you in my arms now and forever and that's all that matters."

A giggle escaped before I could stop it. "That was corny."

"Don't care about that either."

I watched as he reached over for his cell phone, I assumed to check the time.

"I still have time before I need to be in the shower. Which means I have plenty of time to do this."

I squealed as Ace pulled me back down on the bed and maneuvered our bodies so that my body was pinned underneath his. He brushed a piece of my hair out of the way and I watched as his dark eyes studied every part of my face as if committing it to memory.

I expected him to kiss me, given how closely he was studying my lips, but instead, he attacked my neck, finding that exact spot that he knew would make me go wild.

I moaned in delight as my fingers made their way into his short locks in hopes that he would continue his assault. He didn't disappoint. My fingers flew from his head and onto the bed, clenching the sheets as my desire for him grew with every lick, nibble, and bite.

I didn't feel his hand weave its way into my hair until it was too late. He pulled my head to the side, giving him better access to my neck. When Ace removed his hand from my hair, the hand traveled down my body and pushed my thighs open even more than they were. It didn't take much to guess where he might be headed next, and I couldn't stop the tremble that took over my entire body.

Ace shifted his body so that he could move farther south, making a small stop to kiss each nipple before he continued his descent. I watched him under half-opened eyes as my anticipation continued to build as he made his way down my body.

When Ace was eye level with my pussy, he lifted his index finger and slowly moved it down my slit. I lifted my head at the right moment because I watched as he used his fingers to play with me. I swore I heard him mumble something about my pretty pussy before his mouth was on me.

My head flew back onto the pillow as I enjoyed the sensations flying through my body. When his fingers joined the party that his mouth was inflicting on me, I cried out because the feelings that were coursing through my body were too much, but also not enough at the same time. I wanted more, as much as he was willing to give and even that might not be enough.

My groans became more erratic the longer he went on and soon he had enough. His movements quickened, as if he sensed me growing closer and closer to the edge. After I exploded all over his tongue and fingers, he removed his fingers and mouth from me. He stared me down as he sucked his fingers one by one. It might have been the most erotic thing I'd ever seen. I doubted that thought because as soon as he positioned his cock with my pussy, I was done for. He impaled me in one swift motion, and I cried out in pleasure.

He slid into me again and again, and I matched his thrusts with my own. I could feel the pressure building inside me again and I knew it was only a matter of time before I came again. But then he stopped moving.

Before I could take another breath or ask him what was wrong, his lips were on mine and the kiss quickly turned rough. It was obvious that he was the one in control and I was along for the ride wherever it led.

Soon, everything changed. Ace flipped us over, me ending up on top of him. There was a small twinkle in his eyes just before he said, "Fuck me, baby."

His encouragement forced a grin to appear on my face. I adjusted my body and the smile was quickly wiped away when I felt myself ease down on his cock. As I took him, inch by inch, I groaned as the feeling of him inside of me took over. Instead of moving, I embraced our connection, choosing to enjoy the moment instead of moving.

"I thought I told you to fuck me."

His words forced me to look down at him and I said, "This is my show and if I want to sit here with your dick inside of me, I will."

That caused a growl to fall from his lips. "You're determined to be a bad girl today, sweetness."

Our gazes met and I couldn't help the smirk playing on my lips. "Depends on what it gets me. Although I love when you tell me I'm a good girl."

This time, it was Ace's turn to smile at me, but his eyes darkened and I knew it was only a matter of time before he flipped the tables on me. And that could happen quite literally.

I began to move my body and his hands landed on my hips. His eyes were fixated on my tits as he watched them move up and down, following the motions my body was making. The new angle that our bodies created brought a new intensity that I absolutely loved. I also loved seeing his eyes glaze over as I was the one controlling our tempo. It was me that was driving him to the edge this morning and being able to watch him while I was in charge of our pleasure was a sight to behold and the look of pure bliss on his face was something that would be ingrained in my brain forever. I shut my eyes as I shut my mind off again and let my body take over.

When I climaxed for the second time, my body fell limp over Ace's, but he had other plans. I gave him a small smile as he flipped us over again and entered me.

"Yes," I whispered as he picked up the speed as he tried to find his own release as well.

Ace groaned when he came undone and I had no problem with him resting on my body as we both tried to catch our breaths. There would be time for clean up later.

I might regret being up this early later, but for now, it was well worth it.

~

I LAZILY WATCHED as Ace got dressed, wishing that he was doing the opposite. I flipped the blanket covering my naked body back and grabbed the button-down that Ace had discarded the night before. After I buttoned a few buttons to keep the shirt on my body, I walked over to Ace, who was almost dressed.

I straightened his navy tie and smoothed out his suit jacket. I might have been using that as an opportunity to feel him up, but neither of us minded if the smirk on his face was anything to go by.

"We'll both be home before you know it."

I sighed. "I know, and I actually love my job, but I just want to crawl back into bed."

"I understand that feeling completely."

A knock on the bedroom door drew our attention away from one another and I walked out of the line of sight of the door as Ace answered it.

"Sir, your car has arrived."

"Thank you, Anderson. I'll be right down."

Ace closed the door and walked over to me. He pulled me into his arms and gave me a long hug. Neither of us wanted to let go, and finally, with a low growl, Ace took a small step back, ending our connection for the moment.

He smoothed my hair away from my face and tucked it behind my ear before he lifted my chin with his finger.

"Cross Sentinel will be following you on the way to Beyond the Page since I won't be driving you."

"I know. And they'll be out front until it's time for me to leave and then they'll follow me back here until I'm home."

None of this was new anymore, but I thought it was cute that he was reassuring me of my safety. It was something I appreciated *without a doubt and it made me feel better about the situation I was caught in with Falcone. Well, that and Ian being dead.*

Instead of saying another word, he leaned in and kissed me, silencing any thoughts that I might have had. He deepened the kiss and I wondered if he remembered that he had a car waiting on him downstairs, ready to whisk him away to New York City.

This time, I broke our connection and gave him a small smile as my hand landed on his cheek. "You really need to go."

"What are you going to do?"

I turned to look out the window and saw that the sun still hadn't begun to rise. "Probably go back to sleep. It's not even the crack of dawn yet. I'm only up for the sex and to tell you to kick some ass today."

That made Ace chuckle. "Okay, well, I'll see you after work this evening."

"I'll see you then."

Ace stole a quick kiss before he walked out of our bedroom, closing the door behind him. The silence that he left felt weird, but I thought nothing of it. I strolled over to my side of the bed and checked my phone to make sure I'd set an alarm for when I had to be up to get ready for work myself. Once that was done, I crawled back into bed and pulled the covers around me. I felt myself getting drowsy almost as soon as my head hit the pillow and before I knew it, I'd fallen asleep.

2

ACE
PRESENT TIME

I thought about the moment Harlow and I spent together this morning and couldn't stop my grin. Thinking about her and what we would do later tonight was the only thing keeping me somewhat patient until I could pull her into my arms again. I tapped my finger against my knee as I impatiently waited for this ride to end. Though, I should have considered myself lucky that we hadn't gotten stuck in a lot of traffic on the way out of the city. Flashes of how much the scenery changed as I moved from New York City's landscape of tall buildings to upstate New York's greenery were always fascinating to watch.

Normally, I would have stayed in the city after a board meeting. A few members of my team were talking about going to happy hour and I could have made an appearance. We'd rent out a bar or restaurant and allow everyone to order whatever they wanted. It helped keep company morale up and while that occasion was still occurring, today I decided to change gears. Getting to Beyond the Page was the only priority on my list.

Harlow had asked me to text her when the board meeting was done, and I had, but now I had a better idea. Surprising her by arriving at the end of her shift seemed like a better idea and I'd tell her all about the meeting then. I couldn't wait to get back to Harlow and I never thought I would think that about another person. I'd thought about asking if she wanted to join us at my company's celebration, but that would have been a bit much after, I'm sure, the long day she had at the bookstore. And I couldn't deny that I'd also wanted to keep her to myself this evening. That made me think that another vacation sometime soon was in order.

What I had to do was keep in mind that Harlow, now working at Beyond the Page, was important, but the desire to surprise her again was there. Normally, I would do whatever it took to get my way, but I knew I needed to tread carefully here. It was of utmost importance for Harlow to have this job because it was what she wanted. I promised myself I wouldn't overstep any boundaries to harm her chances of being successful at her job.

I made a mental note to myself to talk to Chanel on the side about when might be a good time for Harlow to take off. This was a great idea if I had to say so myself.

There was something else I wanted to do for her as well. I opened up the last text message that I'd sent to Kingston and began typing.

Me: *Can you find out everything there is to find out about Harlow's birth mother? Trying to do this for Harlow. Send me over an invoice when it's all said and done.*

I pressed send and sat back into the car seat. I could do my own search to find her myself, but if Cross Sentinel could start the process at least, it would help speed up the process.

Since I had more time to burn, I checked my calendar to see if there was anything pressing on it. A quick scan showed that there was nothing pressing from work, which was to be expected. What I didn't like was that there was no news on Falcone. Nothing about where he was hiding or what his plans might be. It was almost as if the fucker had vanished off the planet. While that would be a great thought, finding him and being the one to make sure he didn't take another breath was more appealing.

Given that my calendar was lighter now that the board meeting was complete, I not only had a bit more flexibility in when I left for a vacation but also to do more digging into where the hell Falcone was. I trusted that Kingston's men were doing all they could do to find him, even if my patience was wearing thin.

I rubbed my temple slowly as I stared at my phone. Thinking about bringing Falcone an inch away from death and watching him suffer would bring me joy, but not being able to pound his face in right now was giving me a headache.

My mind drifted to seeing my grandfather for the first time in years. Him offering to get a drink with me was odd because we didn't tend to socialize even after I started working for him in the years leading up to his retirement. Why now? Or was this an excuse to talk business like we used to do before he left the country?

Before I could think any more about it, my phone rang. When I tried to answer the call, my calendar app froze and I groaned. *Fucking technology.* It took a few seconds to unfreeze but who was calling finally appeared on the screen. I raised an eyebrow when Harlow's name flashed in front of me. *Odd that she would call me this time of day.*

"Hello, sweetness." I couldn't help but smirk. Had she missed me as much as I missed her?

"Ace." She didn't sound normal. The softness of her voice that I'd grown used to was gone and in its place was fear. Her voice trembled and that raised every hair on my body.

"What's wrong?" I could hear some noise in the background but wasn't able to make out what was going on. Instead, I chose to focus on what she was telling me.

"I'm currently driving the BMW through Brentson," she said. "Emma is chasing me. Please, I need your help now."

The pleading in her voice was almost my undoing. "Fuck! I'm still a ways out. Where the hell are Kingston's men?"

I knew I shouldn't have shouted, but the words flew out of my mouth before I could control them. Yelling right now wouldn't be helpful to Harlow in this situation.

"I don't know, and I'm scared. I'm so damn scared."

"I know, baby. Everything is going to be fine." I leaned over and whispered to my driver. "Change of plans, head toward Beyond the Page, but we aren't stopping there. I'll direct you when we get close to there. Drive as fast as you fucking can."

"But sir—"

If it would have been safe to toss him out of the car and for me to take over driving, I would have. "This is an emergency. Floor it."

He nodded quickly and did as I asked, but nothing could reduce the anxiety and tension I felt until I had Harlow in my arms. When my phone vibrated against my ear, I pulled it away from my ear and put Harlow on speaker. It was a call from Kingston. I couldn't take it because there was no way I was hanging up on Harlow.

Me: *On the phone with Harlow. She's getting chased. What the fuck is going on?*

Kingston: *Long ass story that I'll explain in person. My men are attempting to take out the car following Harlow. Will have an update shortly.*

I looked up and saw that we were about ten minutes away from Beyond the Page. I quickly switched to the tracker that I had on the BMW to get Harlow's location.

"She's gaining on me!"

"Try to remain calm. I just got word that another team from Cross Sentinel is in route and that they aren't that far away. I need you to hold on, baby, okay? Help is on the way."

The sickening feeling that nothing more than my words could calm Harlow crept into my mind. There was nothing I could do other than hope that we got to her location as fast as possible. I watched as we were slowly gaining on the BMW.

"They just hit the back of my car. They're trying to make me crash!"

"Harlow, everything is going to be okay. I promise. I'll be there shortly."

For the first time in a long time, I prayed. My prayers came to a halt when I heard what sounded like screeching tires and metal crunching.

"Harlow!" I shouted, but I got nothing in response except silence because the line went quiet.

3

ACE

My blood turned cold while my heart raced. It was imperative that I kept calm in situations such as this. This wasn't the first crisis I'd been involved in, but this was different. Normally, I was the one in control. Here, I could do absolutely nothing.

"Harlow," I said as calmly as I could muster, but I could hear the slight tremble. "Harlow."

More panic surged through my body. "Harlow!"

The line had gone dead. When I got no response, I looked up. My driver's eyes darted toward the rearview mirror. When our eyes met, his darted back to focus on the road ahead of him. He'd barely avoided the glare I threw his way.

I called her phone and there was no answer. I was holding on to the slim chance that she would answer, but deep down I knew she wouldn't. When Harlow didn't, fear, once again, hit me like nothing I'd ever experienced. *She is gone.*

I hated that my mind went there immediately, but it would make sense with everything that had happened in my life. In fact, it felt poetic in a way. The women that I loved most in my life were taken from me.

My mother's death had been slow and I'd known it was coming. This here was something I'd hoped to prevent and yet my efforts to do so had failed.

Cut it the fuck out. You need to keep it together.

I grabbed the door handle, wishing the logical answer to my issue was to throw open the door and I would appear in front of Harlow where everything would be okay. But that would be a lie.

Time ticked down at a glacial pace as I watched us get closer and closer to the car that Harlow was driving. Every second that went by felt like torture. I tried calling her phone again, but there was no answer. A thought popped into my head. I quickly found Kingston's number because he should be able to give me answers. I should have called him sooner.

"Ace."

Him just saying my name irritated me. "What the fuck is going on? Where is Harlow and where the hell are the guys that were watching her?"

"It's a long story that is better explained in person. We have Harlow and are securing the scene."

My heart dropped. I knew what I thought I heard, but having it slightly confirmed didn't make me feel any better.

"How is she?"

Kingston sighed. "I don't know yet, because we are giving medical professionals the space they need to do their thing. But you need to get here as soon as possible."

"I'm trying." I swiped over to the app I used to track all of my cars and looked. "We aren't far out now."

"Good. If anything changes, I'll call you. If not, I'll see you soon."

I didn't bother saying goodbye, instead choosing to hang up. When I looked up, I saw that we were a block away from Beyond the Page.

"Keep going straight." I glanced down at the tracker again. "I assume we'll come up to a place where there is a car accident on your right."

"Got it, sir."

I hated that my prediction was right. My driver slowed as we came up on exactly what I described. Before my driver could fully stop the car, I was out of it, rushing toward the scene.

There were cars everywhere, lights flashing, and people all around. Most of them looked to be emergency personnel while a few people seemed to be bystanders observing what had happened from a short distance away.

There were two cars that had clearly been in the wreck, matching what Harlow had described in our call. From the direction I was walking up in, I could see part of my BMW's trunk and most of the other car that had been involved in the wreck. Not being able to see more of the vehicle or Harlow enraged me further.

I walked over to the crowd and I watched as they moved out of my way as I walked closer to the accident. Their gazes moved away from the scene in front of them in order to look at me. Their attention on me didn't last long because the real action was unfolding before them.

A guy wearing all black turned to me as I approached and I could see that he was daring me to continue. Too bad that he didn't know I had no intention of stopping.

When I tried to walk past him, he put his hand on my chest. "Sir, you can't go over there right now."

I stared at his hand until he slowly removed it. I dragged my gaze back up to look at him. "The hell I won't."

If he thought he had the ability to keep me from finding Harlow, he had another think coming. Going to jail today wasn't a part of the plan, but if he didn't get the fuck out of my way, I might not be liable for my actions.

His eyes scanned my face for a moment. "Name?"

I huffed and adjusted my stance. He was just doing his job, but it didn't mean I appreciated the annoyance. "Ace Bolton."

He said my name into an earpiece and then nodded. "Mr. Cross will be right over."

It was then I'd realized that there was something slightly off about the emergency personnel that was attending to the scene. When my eyes met Kingston's, it finally clicked. This wasn't Brentson or the neighboring cities. This was Cross Sentinel. That was right, Kingston mentioned they were securing the scene. How the heck hadn't local law enforcement been called in by now?

I couldn't wait for Kingston. If this fucker in front of me wanted to try to stop me, he could make an attempt. There was no way he would succeed.

I glared at him as I walked around him before turning my attention to my car. I walked over to it and saw nothing but a vehicle that looked completely fucked up. The state of the car didn't matter to me. I could buy a million more just like this one.

When I took another step closer, I saw some blood on the airbag that had been deployed. It made me see red. Her blood was shed over this bullshit. I would scorch this entire world to murder the fuckers who caused this.

Getting Falcone was the only thing on my mind outside of Harlow's well-being. I turned my attention to what was left of the car behind my BMW to see if that person was in the car. If the car accident didn't kill them, I would have had no problem finishing the job.

It turned out that it, too, was empty. Maybe they did end up dead and that was better for them than to feel the pain that I'd planned to bring down on them.

"Ace."

I looked to my right and found Kingston standing nearby. It took what felt like less than a second for me to eat up the distance between us.

"Where is Harlow?"

Kingston looked me in the eye before averting his gaze. "She's on her way to the hospital. They left just before you arrived, but I waited for you, so we need to head out now. Here is her phone, which was apparently on her when she was in the accident."

As he handed me the phone, I heard someone shout my name.

"Mr. Bolton!"

I turned and found Chanel, Harlow's new boss, standing by the man who'd stopped me earlier.

"That's Harlow's boss."

Kington nodded. "I know. I was just about to let her through." He waved her over and she came running up to us.

Although she was a distraction from my getting to Harlow faster, her input could be very important.

"I have Harlow's bag. She left it at Beyond the Page."

Since it wasn't found in the car with her, it made sense that it would still be at Beyond the Page. But I knew that Harlow wouldn't go anywhere without her bag. Chanel handed it over to me and I glanced at its contents before putting the phone in it.

When I looked back up at Chanel, I could see that she was fighting back tears. "Do you know what happened?"

I watched as her lip trembled before she could say anything else. "I was busy in the front of the store while Harlow was helping unpack some boxes to restock some books that we needed more of. I heard a crash on our street and ran outside with a bunch of other people that were nearby. There was a car accident near the front of the store. A black SUV was sideswiped."

I assumed that it was Kingston's men who were supposed to be watching Harlow. She tucked her dark-brown hair behind her ear and clasped her hands together. "I don't think anyone was hurt, and the SUV took off down the street, I assume after the car."

I glanced at Kingston and saw a pained look on his face before he closed his eyes. Heads were going to roll and we both knew it. They shouldn't have let Harlow out of their sight.

"I'll explain what happened with that later. It's not good."

I raised an eyebrow at him before turning back to Chanel for her to continue with her version of events.

"I ran into the back to find Harlow but didn't see her. I was about to call the police when a woman named Nikki identified herself as being a member of Cross Sentinel. I remembered the walk-through you gave me after Harlow had been hired and I feared the worst. Nikki brought me here."

Although I wasn't too thrilled about Chanel trusting someone that easily, given what I'd talked to her about before Harlow's first day, it had nothing to do with the car crash. I glanced over her shoulder and found a woman with long red hair tied back into a low ponytail. She nodded at us, acknowledging that we were probably talking about her.

Kingston's hand landed on my shoulder. "We need to head out and get you to Harlow. Nikki can get Chanel's statement."

This wasn't the time or place to discuss it. Lashing out would get me nowhere, so I accepted Kingston's answer. But I also didn't trust Kingston's guys at the moment, even if I'd worked with many of them time and time again. Something had failed here and I was determined to find out what.

"Chanel, if you remember anything or have anything else to share about this, please call this number. I need to get to Harlow."

"I will. I'll also text you, so you have my number. I want to know how Harlow is."

"Of course."

It meant something to me that she cared about Harlow's well-being. I turned toward Kingston and asked, "Are you driving or are you riding with me?"

"I have my SUV right there."

I looked over at the SUV and noticed it wasn't too far away from where the driver I hired was waiting. I stopped by his car, letting him know that his services were no longer needed. Once that was finished, I jogged over to Kingston's car and he pulled away before I could even get the door shut. Once I slammed the seat belt into its buckle, I spoke to Kingston.

"Any updates on her condition?"

"No, and we took her to the nearest hospital. Once she's stabilized, I would suggest transferring her to CIH."

"What the hell is CIH?"

"A private hospital that Cross Industries owns."

This was news to me. "Since when does Cross Industries own a private hospital?"

I watched Kingston's eyes dart over to me before turning his attention back to the road. "Damien bought it after his fiancée was kidnapped and hurt."

I nodded because I remembered hearing about that. I couldn't blame Damien one bit.

Kingston cleared his throat and continued, "You know he hired the best doctors to work there."

"How can I trust your word after what happened this evening?"

At first, Kingston sent a glare my way, but I didn't care. It was a valid point after what had transpired tonight.

"I deserved that but snapping at me isn't going to bring who did this to justice."

Another valid point. "Fine. Once we have her stabilized, I want to have her brought to CIH as long as she gets the best care. I don't care how much it costs."

"Got it."

I stared out at the road in front of me. "Who can you contact right now that will give me more information on Harlow's condition?"

Kingston glanced at the clock on the dashboard. "They should be at Brentson's hospital so it will be difficult to get any information until we get there. We did clear it with hospital staff that we had a VIP victim and they are taking special precautions to protect her identity."

Fair enough. I shifted my questioning. "Do you know who was in the black sedan? Harlow mentioned Emma was in a car chasing her."

"We do have both Emma and the driver of the vehicle in our custody. They were transported to one of Cross Sentinel's facilities."

"How'd you keep the police away from the scene?"

"Friends in high places. Told them we could handle it and didn't want word about what transpired today getting out. Plus, we knew that Mayor Henson didn't want any more trouble in this town."

That made sense. Having this news leak anywhere would be detrimental but I didn't want it to get out to the media. "Now I want you to explain to me how the hell this happened."

4

ACE

"Based on the evidence we've pieced together; this was a planned attack."

"I figured as much if what Chanel said was true."

"She was correct. A number of Cross Sentinel members were in the surrounding area, much like we are in New York City, because we suspected that Falcone might try to use Harlow to get to you. And we were right."

Our conversation was interrupted by Kingston shifting in his seat as he pulled his phone out and put it up to his ear.

I didn't hear much of his conversation because my mind traveled elsewhere. Not knowing Harlow's condition was driving me to the brink. There had been moments in my life where I'd felt like I was spiraling out of control, but they'd occurred years ago. Until today.

Being in control was how I maintained stability in my life. And this was completely out of my hands.

When Kingston hung up, I expected him to start up our conversation once more. He didn't and I grew more anxious.

"If it's bad news about Harlow, I swear I'll—"

"It's not about Harlow, but it is bad news. Two of my men were killed in the pursuit of the other car that was used as a distraction. Another car accident took out all of the passengers in both cars."

"Fuck, man. I'm so sorry."

Kingston wiped a hand across his lips. "It's horrible. After I drop you off at the hospital, I'm going to have to go to their families and tell them that their loved ones have died. Having to do that is one of the worst things in the world."

"I can only imagine." I rubbed a hand over my face and took a deep breath. "I want to pay for their funerals and help in any way I can. It's the least I can do since they died trying to protect Harlow."

"Ace, we provide for our own."

"Let me do this for them. My world is completely fucked up right now and you're already going to have to deal with telling their families that they won't be coming home."

I'd seen some fucked-up things, but I had never had to tell someone that their family member was dead.

Part of me had wanted to tell Kiki Hastings' family that I'd killed her for all the vicious shit she'd done, but I hadn't. As far as I knew, they hadn't been involved in her sick world, but it didn't mean they didn't know about what she was doing. Not that any of it mattered now. She was long gone and while her body burned in the fire I'd set, I hoped her soul burned for eternity in hell.

Instead of hopelessly waiting for Kingston to get to the hospital, I decided to make better use of my time. I pulled out my phone and sent a quick email to my assistant and said I would be out of the office for the rest of the week, if not longer. If there were any emergencies, she knew to forward them to me, but if not, my time was otherwise occupied. Once the email was sent, I called Marnie.

"Yes, sir?"

"Are you still at my house?"

"I am."

"Can you go grab Anderson? I want to tell you both at the same time."

"Okay, give me a moment."

I could hear the hesitancy in her voice. It was rare that I called her on the phone in the time that she'd worked for me.

There was some shuffling around on the other end of the phone and it almost pained me to have to be patient while she found Anderson. I could hear people talking in hushed tones now and I assumed that meant that Marnie had found Anderson.

"Sir? Marnie said you wanted to talk to both of us." Anderson's voice flowed through my phone.

"Yes. I'm going to keep this short, but I want to let you know that Harlow was in a car accident today."

I heard a loud gasp, which I assumed came from Marnie.

There was silence on the other end of the line for a moment before Anderson spoke up again. "Is she okay?"

"I'm not sure, but I should know shortly. I'm on my way to the hospital."

"W-What is it that we can do?"

I glanced at Kingston out of the corner of my eye and thought about what instructions I should leave with them. "I more than likely won't be home tonight, so a change of clothes and toiletries would be great. Essentially a bag that would have all the things I will need if I were going on a business trip because as of now, the hospital will be a home base for me. The same for Harlow because we don't know how long she'll be a patient. Speaking of the hospital, Marnie, would you please meet me at Brentson Hospital?"

The desperation in my voice was foreign. What the hell had I become? I couldn't remember the last time I'd said please to anyone, but this whole situation had made me feel desperate. Desperate to get to Harlow. Desperate to surround her with the people who knew her best.

Harlow loved learning to cook from Marnie and their relationship had started to bloom as a result of their shared love for it. Outside of me, and now Chanel, she'd probably spent the most time with her. Having the people that Harlow trusted around her right now would be crucial and I was determined to give her everything she could possibly need during her recovery... and forever.

When she didn't respond right away, I continued. "I figured since you and Harlow—"

"Of course. I'll be there as soon as I can."

"Thank you."

That phrase hardly came out of my mouth as well. That needed to change too.

"I'll pack your things and drive Marnie to the hospital. I'll also call a car to be ready to pick her up when it's time for her to leave."

That sounded like a good plan. I'd fill Kingston in on what we talked about and we could decide if it made sense to have security at my home and with Anderson and Marnie.

I hung up quickly, not wanting to waste any more of their time. I wanted Marnie to get to the hospital fast and continuing to talk with me on the phone would prolong that.

I debated calling my grandfather. The first people you usually called in a situation like this was your family, but he was practically a stranger to me. Why had I even thought of him? I chalked it up to him appearing in person at the board meeting and the strain I was mentally under.

I ran a hand through my hair, pulling on the strands harder than necessary. If I kept this up, I was going to lose my hair.

"Are you okay? We're almost there."

"Honestly? I'm hanging on by a thread. I've kept people at a distance for this very reason. Caring about someone always has a way of fucking things up."

"You're preaching to the choir on that one."

I knew he was talking about his relationship with his girl-friend, Ellie Winters, which had formed during a time when neither of them was looking for love. In fact, I remembered when I'd delivered the news that Kingston had a half-sister who just so happened to be in Brentson, attending college. What he'd done with that information after I'd given it to him, I wasn't sure.

"Have you told her you loved her?"

I glanced at him out of the corner of my eye, wondering where the hell he was going with this. "Yes, I have."

"Good. This has nothing to do with the situation you're currently in, but—"

I didn't hear the rest of his comment because in my mind, it had everything to do with this. When I told her I loved her before she left for work this morning, it truly might have been the last time. That was something I didn't know if I could live with.

5

ACE

I bolted out of the car before Kingston could come to a full stop. I was barely able to get the words out to tell the receptionist who I was there to see. Thankfully, security had been waiting there and immediately took me to where Harlow was located.

When I stood at the foot of her bed, I couldn't help but stare at her. Knowing what I knew about her injuries, I knew she had to be in pain, but what hit me in the gut was seeing her face bruised. While some of her injuries were obviously visible, including her sprained wrist, seeing her face like this was an even bigger dose of reality about what had happened this evening. It both saddened me and filled me with rage. Every inch of me wished that I could take her place so that she couldn't feel the pain she had to be in.

It hurt me to see her like this. The gown that she had on was the only clothes she currently had because doctors had rushed her in and cut off the things she was wearing. Her being attached to all of these wires that were tracking her vitals. The sounds coming from the machines provided a rhythmic beat that was anything but soothing.

Yes, she was alive, but she'd been knocked unconscious in the accident and still hadn't woken up. Tests were being run to make sure there was no trauma to her head and no internal bleeding or skull fractures. Her doctors had decided to let her rest for now instead of intubating her because of her response to one of the tests was positive.

How she hadn't had more injuries was a blessing after seeing what state the car was left in. There was no doubt in my mind that this could have been so much worse. Although I felt shitty about the events that unfolded, I had to acknowledge some of the positives.

Her sprained arm lay limp on her stomach and I made sure to avoid it as I sat in the chair on the other side of her bed. I thought about her bruised ribs and how they were going to take some time to heal as well. I hated to break this news to her when she woke up, but at least she was alive.

She is alive.

I found myself repeating those words more often than not, almost like a mantra. What had I hoped to achieve by doing it? If I had to be honest, I wasn't sure, but it gave me a temporary reprieve from the guilt and anger that I felt surrounding all of the events of the last few days.

Regret filled my mind as I took in the picture in front of me. I should have been there today. But if Kingston was right and this was all preplanned, then Falcone knew I would be preoccupied with the board meeting. He knew I wouldn't be at Beyond the Page to protect Harlow and had no problem taking out two of Kingston's men to do it.

Son of a bitch.

I softly grabbed her uninjured hand and stared at it in the palm of my own. Seeing her like this felt like someone was strangling my heart. I'd thought I was broken. Any displays of emotion from me were buried long ago.

That was until Harlow.

I lightly squeezed her hand and hoped that she knew I was there by her side. Every step of the way, no matter what happened.

But seeing her like this was too painful to bear. It made me realize how much she had become an intricate part of my life and seeing her this way brought back painful memories that I hoped to keep buried.

Images of how I'd stayed by my mother's bedside as she died before me. Flashbacks of how frail she'd been appeared in my mind even when I tried to force them aside. How much I prayed and promised to do anything in order to have my mom back. To be able to see the vibrant woman she once was outside of memories was all I ever wanted, but unfortunately it wasn't enough.

This wasn't a repeat of that. Doctors were optimistic about Harlow's recovery, whereas there was no doubt in my mind that Mom was going to pass away all those years ago. Although I was happy that Harlow's prognosis was good, the slight optimism faded as I guided my eyes back down to the woman who lay on the hospital bed in front of me. What I wouldn't do for this woman... and to make sure that she was completely happy.

We were going to go on that vacation that I'd planned on surprising her with. I'd already put in motion things that needed to be done in order to make her as comfortable as possible when she was released from the hospital. My priority was to make sure that she was well cared for inside of the hospital as well as when she went home. She would receive anything she wanted or needed.

While a lot of this was materialistic, it was the only thing I could control right now, so I threw my all into it. I wanted nothing more right now than to pull her into my arms and keep her there forever. But first, we needed to make it past this.

"Harlow, I'm not sure if you can hear me but—"

I stopped talking because it felt somewhat foolish to be talking to someone when you weren't sure if they could hear you. But if there was the off chance that she could, it would be worth it.

I cleared my throat and started again. "Harlow, if you can hear me, I just want to tell you how much I love you and that you mean the absolute world to me. I'll keep showing you how much I love you until I take my last breath. Just please wake up."

I stared at her, willing her with my mind to open her pretty eyes and give me a small smile. Her laughter filled my heart with joy. Not being able to hear it again would tear me to pieces and would be something I'd never recover from. I would throw away all of the money I had just to see her do it. But she didn't.

When I leaned down and rested my forehead on our joined hands, I could feel wetness gathering in the corners of my eyes. I didn't bother repositioning my body because I knew that the inevitable would happen.

I didn't know how long I'd stayed that way, but my sore neck told me I'd stayed in that position for far too long. It forced me to readjust my body. Although I didn't want to let her hand go even for a moment, I did in order to stretch and hopefully remove the crick that was now in my neck.

My phone started vibrating and I reached into my pocket to send the call to voice mail. Whoever it was could wait. I wasn't in the right frame of mind to talk to anyone and I didn't want anyone to hear the anguish that I was sure would be in my voice.

The range of emotions that I'd felt throughout the course of the last few hours finally crashed down on me like a ton of boulders. Coming off a big high from the board meeting to hitting what I deemed was the deepest of lows had been rattling around in my mind for days, but it had finally taken its toll physically. I'd tried to fight it for as long as I could, but this battle within myself was lost. For the first time in a long time, I cried.

6

ACE

"I'm going to speak out of turn here because I've seen you suffer for long enough."

I looked up from my laptop and turned to face Marnie, wondering where this was going. I'd never had any issues with her. She had always done her job diligently and had worked with my grandfather for so many years and now for me. But the tone of her voice had me questioning that decision.

It was a couple of days later and I'd been able to get Harlow transferred to Cross Industries Hospital. Marnie had come to visit her every day since the accident. I allowed her to stay in one of the guest bedrooms in the penthouse I bought so that her commute to the hospital wouldn't be nearly as long as it would be from my estate. Although we mostly sat with each other in silence, me working on my computer and her knitting something, I liked having someone else around even if we sat in comfortable silence.

That was until now.

"This is another traumatic event for you. Losing your

mom at a young age would be rough on anyone. It would be hard for most people to deal with and they would need guidance to help them through the trauma."

If only she knew the half of it.

Wait. Maybe she did. Marnie had been my grandfather's cook before she became mine. She'd been working for Boltons for two decades and had worked for a friend of my grandfather's before that. There might be a slight chance...

"You know, you're right. Do you remember anything?"

"Not a whole lot. I had only been working for your grandfather for maybe a year when your mom died."

"I know, still maybe you overheard something. Did you hear anything related to my mother's death?"

It felt foolish asking about this when my attention should have been solely on Harlow's recovery. But something deep inside of me refused to let this go, even temporarily. Maybe it was because I felt the most vulnerable that I'd ever felt in my life.

"I haven't. Now that we've gotten that cleared up, why don't you go and take a short break, get some air or something and I'll sit here with Harlow. If she wakes up, I'll call you immediately."

I trusted Marnie. That was evident by my not firing her when I took over my grandfather's estate. She'd worked for him because he paid her handsomely and not because of the man himself. Based on what I knew, she barely saw him anyway and that was probably what she preferred.

I stared at Harlow once more, wishing she would open her eyes.

Wake up, sweetness. Wake up.

When she didn't, I turned away and walked out of the

hospital room. I glanced down at my visitor's badge on my chest before taking in my surroundings. Thankfully, no one was around and I didn't need to deal with anyone trying to make small talk with me when I didn't feel like talking as I headed outside.

I sucked in all the air that I could. It felt as if it was the first time that I'd taken a breath since Harlow called me.

The saying that things could change in the blink of an eye had never rung truer in my life. The guilt I felt buried any relief that I had about Harlow surviving the car accident because all of this was because of me. Trusting Cross Sentinel was what I chose to do and the fault didn't lie with them. It was a decision that I made and I failed her.

I knew there were obligations that I had to take care of, including interrogating Emma and the other asshole that had caused the car chase and the resulting car crash, but I couldn't bring myself to do it. I needed to know for sure Harlow was out of the woods.

I would give anything just to see her smile again.

The way our relationship began was tragic. Time had been wasted. We could have spent that time getting to know each other and building something together instead of arguing and fighting for the upper hand. It would have meant more time I could have spent with her.

I couldn't help but think about the time we lost when she left my home and hid, only for Ian to find her. But it had led her back into my arms and got that fucker off the streets. Then again, if none of this had happened, would I have ever met her?

Here I was, standing outside of a hospital, feeling like shit after all of the things that had happened over the last few months. Maybe if I hadn't attended the board meeting, I could have saved her because, in the grand scheme of things, the meeting meant absolutely nothing.

After another deep breath, I turned around and walked back into Cross Industries Hospital. I had to admit that Damien Cross had outdone himself when he bought this hospital. It had innovative technology and some of the best doctors in their respective fields. I knew that Harlow was getting some of the best care in the world.

It had taken some research and convincing on both Kingston and Damien's part to get me to move Harlow, but after talking to Dr. Grace McCartney, who would be one of the doctors overseeing Harlow's care, I was grateful that Brentson Hospital was willing to transfer her without any issues.

Instead of heading up the elevator to Harlow's room, I decided to grab a drink. I walked into the cafeteria and it took me a bit longer than I would ever admit to anyone to order a coffee. Ordering one this late in the day wouldn't do me any favors, but it wasn't as if I was planning on going to sleep anytime soon anyway. I took a sip and closed my eyes. Damien didn't skimp here either because the coffee tasted divine.

I walked back toward the elevator and watched as the numbers slowly changed, indicating that I was one floor closer to where Harlow was resting. When I appeared in the doorway, Marnie looked up and gave me a small smile. Before I could walk in, my phone rang.

I held up a finger and turned around before looking at the screen. It was a call from Kingston and I knew that I had to take it.

I walked over to a window down the hall and answered, "Ace."

"We found two more guys that were involved with trying to kidnap Harlow. No one is talking yet and we don't know who hired them, but some of the methods that we use can be... very persuasive."

"I know. I've seen you at work."

"I don't normally take orders from other people, but this is your deal."

I cleared my throat. "Hold them until Harlow wakes up. She's my top priority and I'm not dealing with any more shit until I know she's going to be okay. If that means they stay wherever you have them for years, so be it."

"Understood. I'll keep you updated if any of them talk."

"Good."

"That wasn't the only news I had. We've had a Falcone sighting."

My eyes narrowed at the sound of his name. "Where is he?"

"Miami. Apparently, he felt the need for a vacation."

I bet he did. "Does Will and the Vitale family know about this?"

"We got the information from them."

Fuck. "We can't have them find Falcone first. That fucker is mine."

"I know, which is why I've had Cross Sentinel's Miami office looking into every possible way we can track him. We had a feeling he might have left the city because he'd been too quiet and the feelers we put out on him turned up empty."

Any news on Falcone was welcome, but I couldn't stop

this thought from flying out of my mouth. "Isn't it awfully strange that now we get a tip about him? He's been in the wind, for what?" I paused to think about how long we'd been searching for him.

"It has been weeks now. And this is a time where he just so happens to be spotted? I can't help but be suspicious because I don't believe in coincidences."

"Neither do I. I wouldn't be surprised if he finally wanted to be found."

"But why now?"

"And that's the billion-dollar question. Is everything going well at Cross Industries Hospital? How is Harlow doing?"

I sighed before I could help myself. "No real changes, unfortunately."

"But at least the transition to Cross Industries Hospital went seamlessly. Damien made sure of it."

That I could agree with. I turned away from the window for a moment and found Damien Cross walking toward me.

"Funny you should mention him. Your cousin is walking toward me as we speak."

"Not surprising. I assume he wanted to check in to see how things were going. Tell him I said hello."

I scoffed. "Because I don't have anything else better to do."

Our banter made me smile for the first time in days. Instead of waiting for Kingston to say something else, I hung up and gave my full attention to the man approaching me. And he wasn't alone.

A woman with long dark hair stood next to him, her arm looped through his with a diamond ring on display. The other hand held a bouquet of colorful flowers.

"Thank you for everything, Damien," I said as I held my hand out for him to shake.

He returned the gesture and said, "Of course. If there is anything else we can do, I'll make it happen."

And I knew he would.

He glanced at the woman standing next to him and cleared his throat. "Excuse me. This is Anais, my fiancée."

Once again, I held out my hand, this time for her to shake.

She gave me a small smile as we shook hands before she said, "Happy to meet you. I'm so sorry that all of this happened."

Anais glanced down at her hand before looking back at me. "These are for Harlow. Hopefully they might bring some happiness to her when she wakes up."

A tinge of jealousy began to crowd my judgment. Seeing Damien with the love of his life, while mine was fighting for hers, forced me to fight back my emotions. Emotions I thought had been buried forever lay just below the surface, threatening to reveal my true feelings.

I'd trained myself not to show emotions. It came in handy during the time I'd lived with Kiki, and I allowed myself to dig back into that frame of mind now to avoid causing a scene. Keeping a clear head right now was crucial, no matter what I was going through internally.

"It's horrible, but we'll make it through. Once Harlow is in a good place in her recovery, I'm going to get that son of a bitch."

"I have no doubt in my mind that you will. I understand the situation you're in, unfortunately, and I would do the same."

I watched the tender look he gave his fiancée before his eyes focused back on me. I couldn't help but wish that I'd be able to see the same look in Harlow's eyes that was reflected in Anais's.

Shake it off, Ace. Now isn't the time.

"You seem to be closer to Will than most. I don't know how much information he is passing on to Kingston, but if you can find out anything, that would be great."

Damien nodded. "Sure. The Cross Family has a stake in this now that two of Kingston's men have died because of it."

Anais gasped beside him. I guess he hadn't mentioned it to her.

"We didn't want to intrude for too long, so we're going to go, but here's my card with my number on it to reach me directly."

"Thank you for coming."

Damien dipped his head before turning toward his fiancée. Anais leaned over to give me a quick hug and I was surprised by the gesture. Damien narrowed his eyes in response and I shook my head. He was overprotective and I didn't blame him one bit.

Together they walked away and I was left staring at their backs, holding the flowers for Harlow. This present would join the roses I'd bought and the ones that Chanel sent early this morning.

I needed to talk to someone who would have current information on Falcone. I ran through my mental Rolodex and one name appeared above the rest: Parker Townsend.

7

ACE

I mumbled several cuss words under my breath when I tried the same thing for the third time and got the same result. I'd found Parker's cell phone number from when we arranged the last-minute meeting where he handed me the papers about my grandfather. Calling the man three times in a row should have meant that this was an emergency or that I was desperate. In reality, it was both and I was irritated that he hadn't answered.

Realistically, I understood that he was a very busy man and there could be a number of reasons why he hadn't answered his phone. None of those did anything to help me feel better about it.

Instead, I walked back into the room and sat down at Harlow's bedside. Marnie didn't bother trying to engage in small talk and it wasn't until we heard a knock on a door that anyone said anything.

We both looked toward the door and found Kingston standing there with an angry look on his face.

"I thought you left after you dropped me off."

"I did until I got a call that the asshole who hit Harlow's car with his own vehicle needed medical attention. Apparently, he slipped and fell."

I crossed my arms. "Did he 'slip and fall' or was he helped to the ground while he was in your custody?"

When Kingston shrugged, I had my answer.

"We thought it was best to bring him to minimize any attention that he might draw and it made the fucker suffer a bit more having to drive from Brentson into the city. Do you want to go talk to him?"

I glanced back at Harlow and how peaceful she looked right now. I didn't want to leave her, but if a conversation with this prick would get me a step closer to finding the fucker who put this hit out on her, it was well worth it. Plus, with Parker in the wind, this might be one of the few opportunities I had to find out more information and I wasn't about to waste it.

This time, I turned back to Marnie and said, "You're okay with me leaving again?"

She nodded. "If it means getting whoever did this, then by all means go. It's a shame that she or anyone would have to go through this."

I agreed with her, but while many people might have to wait for justice, I refused to anymore. I'd waited long enough to get back at Kiki and my patience was gone now.

"If anything changes—"

"I'll call you or have someone page you. Go on. She's in good hands."

My eyes lingered on Harlow's form for a moment before I tucked a piece of hair behind her ear and leaned down to kiss her forehead. I watched her once more before I stepped away.

I followed Kingston into the elevator where I found myself staring at the closed doors, preparing myself for what might happen when I entered the room. I rolled my shoulders back and clenched and unclenched my fists. The urge to fight whoever this was and to hurt them to the point where they'd beg me to pull the trigger was high. I probably could get away with it, but I needed to get any information that I could get out of him first.

I glanced at Kingston out of the corner of my eye and found him staring back at me. "What?"

"Nothing. Just making sure that you're okay."

"I'm as fine as can be given what is going on."

Kingston shrugged his shoulders and I could see that he didn't believe me. He was right, though, but I wouldn't admit it out loud. I wasn't fine and I wouldn't be fine until Harlow walked out of this hospital under her own power.

When the elevator reached the floor that we wanted, I took a deep breath. Not for nerves, but to try to curb the feelings that were bubbling deep inside of me. As I walked down the hall with Kingston, several of the hospital's employees looked at me, and I couldn't help but wonder what they thought of me. Did I look like I could commit murder? If any of the rage I was building snapped, I didn't know what I would be capable of and I wondered if the people I passed could feel that too.

We reached an unnumbered door with a guard standing outside of it. The man nodded at Kingston before moving to the side, allowing Kingston and me to walk in. Inside the hospital room, which paled in comparison to the one Harlow was in, lay a man with a bandage on his forehead looking at the wall. There was another guard in there with him, I assumed to take extra precautions in case he attempted to escape. The guard looked up at us as we entered the room, but the patient didn't. Unless his hearing had been fucked up in the car accident, there was no way he didn't hear us enter.

I cleared my throat and the prick in the bed still didn't turn around to acknowledge our existence. I walked over to the bed and yanked his face so that he was facing me. He winced in pain and his hurting made me smile on the inside.

"Who are you?"

"Jeremy."

"Who hired you?"

The man turned away, as if he couldn't be bothered to look at me, but he did answer. "I don't know."

"How the hell don't you know who hired you?"

"Because I don't."

My hand gripped the hospital bed railing and it took all of the control inside of me not to try and flip it with this fucker on it.

"How about you tell me what you do know?"

This time he glanced at me on his own but said nothing.

"I won't say anything if he just so happens to die in this bed."

"No, we can save that for later. I don't want the doctors, nurses, and other medical professionals in this building to have to deal with any more of his bullshit. I'll wait until he's released and then force him to suffer all over again."

When his hand shook as he brought it to his jaw, I knew I'd gotten him. None of this shit was a game, but if he wanted to play, then, by all means, I'd play.

"Fine, I'll tell you what I know. Emma told me that she had a job for me that would be easy money and she only needed a couple of hours of my time, but I don't know who hired her. All I had to do was drive her to a bookshop in Brentson, drop her off and then wait for her to return. That's all I know, okay? I wasn't planning on any of the other bullshit that happened."

"Did you know anything about another black sedan being in the area?" This time, it was Kingston asking the questions. I assumed he wanted to close some loopholes about what happened to two of his men that were killed in the accident.

He shook his head. "Nope. What I was hired to do was what I already told you. I didn't expect the rest of this shit to happen."

I looked at Kingston. "Do we have any reason to believe he's not telling the truth?"

Kingston glanced at Jeremy. "No, but we will find out if he's lying. And if he is..." His voice trailed off, leaving room for interpretation.

The look Kingston gave me said enough. And it must've been enough for Jeremy because he spoke again with a quiver in his voice. "Look, I swear I told you all I know. I was told to pick Emma up at one location and to drop her off at another location."

"I want the addresses to those locations. Did you pick the car up from a different location or was it at the first address?"

"It was at the first location. I was told to meet her there and she had the car keys. My phone should be in those jeans over there. That has the addresses of where I was supposed to pick up and drop off along with the address of the bookshop."

It took no time for me to eat up the space between me and the clothes he laid on a chair on the other side of them. His phone was where he said it was and I looked at him and raised an eyebrow. "What's your passcode?"

"Three-seven-nine-four-four-one."

I pressed the numbers on the keypad and it worked. "Was it sent via text message or through email?"

"Text. Her number is in my phone, so it should be under Emma."

Once again, I proved his information to be factual because I did find the text message and the corresponding addresses. I scanned the text to confirm that was all that was said before handing it over to Kingston.

"I'll send someone over to these places right away."

"If this information checks out, you might have just saved your life."

Jeremy swallowed hard. "Thank you. All I was trying to do was make some money. I swear I didn't think all the rest of this would happen."

"But you were the one driving the car that hit Harlow's vehicle."

"I—I didn't mean to hit her so that she spun out, I swear. It was just to stop her and—"

"Kidnap her."

His face grew pale as he realized his answers were only proving how involved he truly was in this whole stunt.

I was starting to believe him in that while he was a willing participant, he didn't mean for all of this to go awry. Then again, you could never be too sure. Trusting anyone right now was not on the top of my list. Hell, part of me was still pissed at Kingston, even if his explanation made sense.

"Does that mean you'll let me go when I get out of here?"

"I'm not saying that, but I do appreciate the information you've given us."

I knew my words meant nothing and that was his problem, not mine. With a quick nod at Kingston, I walked out of the hospital room, this time, with him following behind me. Once the hospital room door was closed behind us and we'd walked back toward the elevators, I finally spoke.

"How long will it take your men to reach these locations?"

"They're on their way now, so within the hour. I have some of my people trying to find everything there is to know about the history of the two addresses and who owns the property now."

"Good. Keep me in the loop because I want to know ASAP."

"Of course. And what do you want me to do about Jeremy?"

"Whatever you want. He means nothing to me. My focus is on Harlow and Harlow alone until she gets out of here."

When the elevator heading up stopped at our floor, I hopped on.

"Ace?"

I didn't bother turning around, instead choosing to look over my shoulder at Kingston.

He waved his hand in front of the elevator doors to prevent them from closing before he spoke. "Cross Sentinel wants to find out who did this just as bad as you do. We lost two of our own, so whatever blame you lay at our feet about what happened makes sense and I'm truly sorry for it. But know that we won't stop until this is over and done."

I nodded. "Understood."

The elevator doors closed behind me.

8

HARLOW

I could hear a faint, dull noise in the distance. *What is that sound?*

I couldn't place it, no matter how hard I tried. Annoyance was building because the sound was growing louder, but still I didn't know what was making that noise. *Why can't I tell where the sound is coming from?*

I tried to open my eyes, but they felt as if something was holding them down. The noise was growing louder. I tried to shift my attention away from the beeping and pay attention to my eyesight. If I could open my eyes, I could identify what the hell that noise was. However, it was easier said than done. The effort it took to open my eyes took a toll on me and I felt myself growing tired, but I didn't want to give in. I needed to know where that noise was coming from.

When I was finally able to free my eyes, I squinted. The lights in the room were too much, but I refused to give in. All I could see was a sea of white before I shut them once more. After what I thought was a few seconds, I forced myself to slowly open them and although it was hard for me to focus, I recognized the figure sitting next to me immediately.

Ace. I blinked hard before I opened my eyes again. He was still there and not a figment of my imagination. I didn't trust my voice, so I just stared at the handsome man before me.

It took a few moments for me to gather the courage to speak. When I finally did, only one word fell from my lips. "Hey."

My voice sounded hoarse, making me regret the decision to speak. I swallowed hard, trying to coat my dry throat. It didn't work. I winced when I took a deep breath. That hurt like hell and I almost wished I didn't have to do it again, but that would mean I was dead.

Ace jumped slightly before his eyes met mine. A small smile played on his lips before he pushed his chair back, stood up, and walked over to me. He stood near my bedside and just stared at me, taking in every detail of my face. I closed my eyes briefly to give them a small rest before opening my eyes again.

Ace waited for me to open them before he leaned down toward me. He gently rested his head on mine. The smallest touch from him was enough to make me try to smile even through the pain.

"I love you."

My mind still felt cloudy and my head hurt. But having those be the first words that I heard in what felt like a long time was music to my ears. I swallowed hard again before I said, "I love you too."

"You don't know how long I've been waiting to hear you say that."

His response puzzled me. What did he mean? What was I missing?

One thing I was certain of was that my head was throbbing and my throat felt scratchy. I looked down and saw that my left wrist was wrapped up. What the hell had caused that? I could feel my heart rate starting to race as I took in my surroundings. I took a deep breath to try to calm down, but I winced. Something that I took for granted every day now hurt to do.

"Be careful. You bruised a couple of ribs in the car accident."

"Car accident? Where am I?" My voice cracked and I tried to swallow again, encountering the dryness in my mouth once more.

Ace ran a hand down my cheek. The warmth from his hand soothed me. It felt as if it had been years since I felt his touch. "Can I get you some water? I have a water bottle and there is a straw over there."

I nodded and cleared my throat as he opened the water bottle and put a straw into it. When the room temperature water hit my throat, I breathed a sigh of relief. I closed my eyes as the water made its way through my body. I opened them again and took another sip.

"I'm okay for now. Thank you."

Ace put the water bottle on the bedside table. "You're in the hospital."

That realization made me panic. I wasn't able to move fast, but I felt my heart start to race. "I—I'm where?"

The question fell off my lips before I had a chance to connect the dots. Car accident, hospital... I tried hard to remember anything related to an accident, but I was drawing a blank.

"Don't stress yourself out over this. All that matters now is that you're safe and recovering."

"I still don't understand. Car accident?" My voice trailed off and I closed my eyes again. It felt good to rest them.

"I'll explain everything once you get a little more rest, okay? Right now, I'm going to call the doctor so that she can speak to you."

I nodded my head and instantly regretted it. I moaned as I tried to adjust my body and felt Ace put his hands on me, halting my movement.

"Don't move too much until Dr. McCartney comes in."

I open my eyes a crack again and look at Ace. Seeing his face almost broke me. It reminded me of the life we had begun to build together, him telling me that he loved me, and all that we'd been through. If I had been in a car accident, I was grateful to have those memories and somewhat thankful that I couldn't remember the car accident. I could only imagine how scared I was during the ordeal, but I wished I could remember why I was in a car accident to begin with.

I shifted my gaze and found beautiful bouquets of flowers sitting on a table near the window. The bright yellows, pinks, purples, and blues brought more color to the room.

I hadn't seen when or how he'd alerted the doctor, but none of that matters now as I opened my eyes wider to look at the woman standing in front of me.

"Hi, I'm Dr. Grace McCartney and I'm one of the doctors that has been taking care of you during your stay at Cross Industries Hospital."

"Okay," I said slowly, still not trusting my own words.

Ace reached over and grabbed my non-bandaged hand as we waited for Dr. McCartney to continue.

"You have a concussion, sprained wrist, and bruised ribs after the car accident you were in. No internal bleeding, thankfully. The bruising on your face will heal with time as well."

I closed my eyes and digested the news. My being involved in a car accident meant that none of this should have been a surprise. Frankly, I was happy to have just made it out alive.

"We want to keep you for a few more days and if everything goes well, we can discuss when to discharge you."

That made sense and frankly, I didn't feel comfortable going anywhere else. My mind drifted slightly, but a light squeeze of my hand from Ace brought my attention back to the situation at hand.

"Dr. Boise will be in at any moment to check on you."

I nodded and shut my eyes as the pain moved through my head. I pleaded with myself for it to end quickly.

"Try to rest, Harlow."

"I will," I whispered. "And I'm sure that he'll make sure that I do too."

Ace smiled down at me, but it did little to mask his true feelings. I could see the sadness mixed with the rage in his eyes. The thoughts that must have been careening through his mind had to have been dark and twisted. I feared for whoever would be on the receiving end of his wrath.

9

HARLOW

I looked over at Ace after he chuckled at a show we were both watching on the television in my room. It felt like the most normal thing in the world and if I had to be in the position I was in right now, I wouldn't want to spend it with anyone else. He was my rock during this entire ordeal, but there was one thing I needed to know and he was one of the only people that could provide me with answers.

"Ace?" My voice was just above a whisper. I couldn't help but be nervous about what I might uncover.

"Hmm?" Ace drew his attention away from the television and over to me.

His gaze danced over my face while he waited for me to respond.

"I want to talk about the accident."

Ace sat up straighter in the chair he was in. His stare never left me, but I could see the wheels in his head turning. I didn't blame him for wondering how to approach this topic.

"Are you sure you want to talk about this right now?"

I nodded, feeling more comfortable with the situation at

hand. "I wasn't feeling up to it yesterday because I had just woken up, but I think I'm ready to hear about it today. I do remember what I think are parts of it, but I'm not sure if I dreamed it or if it was real."

"Well, we can start from where you remember and I'll try to help confirm what I can. It might take some digging to find out everything that happened that day, but I promise I'll do everything in my power to get the answers that we both want and to make sure that justice is served."

My eyes widened slightly before returning to normal. There was no doubt in my mind that Ace's definition of justice and your everyday definition of justice were not the same.

"I remember being in the back room of Beyond the Page, getting books or something to stock some shelves." I paused and looked at Ace, who nodded.

"Chanel confirmed that was what you were doing."

Ace's confirmation made me feel slightly better about my recollection of events, but there was still a lot more to be told.

"I wasn't paying a whole lot of attention, if I'm being honest, to my surroundings, so I didn't hear Emma enter the room until it was too late. I'd wondered how she'd gotten in and how the bodyguards that were watching me hadn't seen her, but there wasn't anything I could do about that at the time."

Ace adjusted his body once more and clenched his fist. I reached for his hand and placed mine over his to hopefully calm him down. It seemed to do the trick because he unclenched his fist. "Another car was hired to distract your security team and they went after them and called a backup team to come to you. The other team didn't come quickly enough and that was how Emma got in. Your original security team was killed in a separate car accident along with the men who caused the distraction."

My eyes widened at his words and I could feel tears forming in the corners of my eyes. That wasn't the news I expected him to say and I felt terrible about the men who'd lost their lives trying to protect me. Ace grabbed my hand in a sign of comfort and I graciously took it.

It took some time for me to calm my emotions, but when I did, I said, "I think I'm okay to continue."

"Are you sure?"

I nodded and then spoke. "Emma looked rough, to say the least. Probably worse than I look now."

Ace gave me a pointed look and I smirked in return. Laughter was supposed to be the best medicine and maybe it was in bad taste to make fun of my current condition and the news I'd just heard. But what was done was done, and what I said was well worth the look that Ace gave me.

I was dejected when I finally got a look at myself in the mirror yesterday. The bruises were brutal and even though I knew they would fade with time, seeing my face marred in different colors was an experience I hoped to never have again.

But I kept telling myself that it could have been much worse than what it was. I knew I was lucky to be alive and was grateful for the opportunity to touch my face again, no matter what its current state was.

"Anyway, Emma told me that I was coming with her because there was somewhere we had to go. She held me at gunpoint, so I knew the chances of me potentially getting away were slim. Emma noticed when I tried to alert Cross

Sentinel on my phone, so that failed. I remember hoping that they would barge in and save the day like you see in the movies, but it didn't happen."

I paused again to gather my thoughts. Ace didn't say anything, instead choosing to patiently wait for me to continue.

"I think I did something to distract Emma..."

"Chanel told a member of Cross Sentinel that there was a huge mess in the back room near the exit. Cardboard boxes were everywhere."

I snapped the fingers of my uninjured hand before placing my hand back over Ace's. "That's right. I must have knocked them over as a way to slow Emma down. It just so happened that I forgot to put the BMW's car key in my purse because I was hurrying to help Chanel due to having more customers than usual at opening. Thankfully I had forgotten to, so I had it with me and was able to drive away... and that's all I remember. Did the car accident look bad?"

Ace didn't say words, but his nod told me all I needed to know. I didn't know if I'd be ready to ever see photos of the accident and thankfully, we didn't have to go into that now.

"Do you remember calling me on the phone?"

I glanced up at the ceiling before looking back at Ace. "Maybe? After leaving Beyond the Page, what I remember becomes blurry."

Ace moved his hand so that my palm was resting in his. "Your version of events fits with the parts that I know."

The way he said it made me think that there was more to the story than he was letting on. "What aren't you telling me?"

"Emma and an accomplice were captured by Cross

Sentinel at the scene of your car accident. I'll find out what she says and compare."

"Why haven't you gone to see them already?" I asked.

"I saw him because he ended up in the hospital but haven't seen Emma yet. Wanted to make sure you were okay first. Making sure that you're safe and out of the hospital is the most important thing to me. Cross Sentinel has her and if she does speak, then we can move things up."

Ace rubbed my cheek with the back of his hand. I leaned into his touch and then said, "I think you need to talk to her as soon as possible. I want everyone who orchestrated this to pay for what they've done."

"I'm not leaving you here alone."

"Is Marnie coming today? Not that I want to drag her here if she doesn't want to come... I'm also okay with being alone for an hour or two."

Ace watched me as he pulled out his phone. I assumed he was going to make the arrangements to talk to her. I watched him work for a few moments before I spoke up again.

"What if she lies about it? She's not the most trustworthy person in the world, as you and I both know."

"If she does, she'll suffer the consequences. Hell, if I find out she's being truthful, she's going to suffer for what she did to you."

"Fair. Are you going to see her tonight?"

He answered my question with one word. "Yes."

10

ACE

"I'm outside the location you told me to meet you at," I said as I stared up at the brownstone in front of me. This was the first time I felt comfortable enough to leave the hospital and that had only happened because Harlow had insisted. It also didn't hurt that the hospital wasn't too far away from where Kingston had asked me to meet him. Although I knew why I was meeting Kingston, why he'd chosen this place confused me. Through some of the assignments I'd worked on with Kingston I'd found myself in many different situations and locations. But never had I been here. Given the purpose of my visit, this was the last thing I expected.

"I'll let you in in a second. Meet me near the door that leads to the basement," Kingston said.

"Okay."

I ended the call. Just before I could step out of my black sedan, my cell phone vibrated in my hand.

"About time you called me back," I said, not bothering to waste any time with friendly greetings or introductions. The irritation was evident in my voice, and I didn't care. My patience was wearing thin.

"You do realize that I don't answer to you, nor do I owe you an explanation."

"Parker, I don't give a damn about where you were or what you were doing. But you might be the key to cracking this case wide open and help me find Falcone."

"Is that what this is about?"

Instead of answering his question straightforwardly, I answered with another question. "I assume you heard about Harlow's accident?"

"I had, but I also assumed that you had taken care of whoever did it."

"My main priority was making sure that she was okay, and now that she is, I'm determined to find Falcone and make him pay for this."

"And you're sure he did this?"

"He's the only one I could think of that would have enough of a motive to. And this wouldn't be the first time that he has tried to harm her. He let one of his goons go after her twice now."

Parker's silence on the other end of the line was unsettling, but I didn't have time to dwell on it. I needed him to either give me the information he had or to find it as quickly as possible.

"What do you need on Falcone?"

I'd been waiting for him to say something along those lines. "I want to know where he is. Cross Sentinel has people on the ground looking for him, but so far, the only time he's been spotted was in Miami, and it was by the Vitale crime family. They're also looking for him, and I want to catch his ass before they do."

"Understandable. Well, I haven't put any feelers out for him yet, but I'll see if I hear anything and maybe find out if he's purchased any property under some of the accounts I know he has."

"Cross Sentinel already looked into that as far as I know."

"Cross Sentinel has some of the best technology and best people working for them to hunt down people. I have the ability to go beyond their scope, as I'm sure you know, or you wouldn't have called me and asked for my help. And you know this won't be free."

I'd been waiting for him to say that. "What do you want in return?"

"I want to know everything that you know about Kiki Hastings and how you killed her."

I debated with myself about how I should answer this demand. Acting as if I didn't know what he was talking about would be fruitless because I knew how resourceful he could be when he wanted to get information. No one else outside of the people that were involved knew that I killed Kiki, which made me wonder if Parker knew that I did it or was insinuating that I had.

I second-guessed my choice just before I said it. "I don't know what you're talking about."

Yes, it was a cowardly response, but I couldn't be too sure.

"Are you saying you had nothing to do with Kiki burning alive in a car in the middle of nowhere? You really don't know how that happened?"

"Parker, you and I both know Kiki had a lot of enemies in this world, it could have been anyone."

"I think it was you."

"You think, or do you know?" I checked the time on my dashboard and looked up to see if Kingston was looking for me, but I saw no one.

"Confirm this for me or I won't do anything regarding Falcone." The desperation in his voice was something new. I didn't know Parker well, but I'd never known him to get rattled by something that seemed inconsequential, especially because Kiki was dead.

"I know what happened to Kiki Hastings." Saying her name made my blood boil, but I refused to take my eyes off of the mission at hand.

"Good. Meet me at the Chevalier headquarters tomorrow at eight p.m."

Parker hung up before I could respond and I found myself staring out the window in confusion. If whatever he had up his sleeve led me closer to Falcone, then I couldn't give a shit less about anything else.

I stepped out of the car before locking the doors and walked up to the brownstone and then around the front stairs toward where I assumed a door to the basement was located. When I reached the first step, the door opened and there stood Kingston, who moved his body to let me into the basement.

Before he could say anything, I whispered, "Had a call with Parker. We might have more information about Falcone's whereabouts tomorrow."

Kingston nodded, understanding why I'd been delayed. The basement was nothing like what I'd imagined it to be based on what I saw when looking at the house from the outside. The outer appearance of the home appeared to be well kept but the basement was the opposite. The basement was very cold and had only a table and a few chairs. I stood in front of the only table. It reminded me of a police interrogation room in a television series drama.

"We'll bring her out in a second. She was not nearly as forthcoming with information as Jeremy, but we thought that (a) you'd want to see her and (b) maybe your presence would change her mind about talking."

"She better start talking."

"We'll see. What I do know is that she's refused to eat any of the meals we provided for her because she's on a hunger strike. She must be starving."

There was a commotion upstairs and I looked over to a set of stairs that led to the upper floors. When the door at the top of the stairs swung open, it didn't take long for Emma to walk down the stairs, followed by two burly men that I didn't recognize, but the assumption that they were with Cross Sentinel was probably the most valid.

One of the men dragged her to sit on the other side of the table. I stared at the pathetic woman in front of me. Emma, or whatever name she was going by this week, looked weaker than the last time I'd seen her, but I contributed that to her lack of food. She'd decided that she was going to go on a hunger strike and while that was her right, there were consequences to that choice.

When her eyes met mine, I couldn't help the thrill that raced through me. I saw fear for a split second. The mask that she threw on to hide her true feelings might work to fool some of the other people in this room, but I wasn't fooled.

I stared her down, daring her to speak first. Although I did want to get this over with and get back to Harlow as

quickly as possible, I had no problem waiting her out until I
got what I wanted.

"You don't have better food?"

"I heard you were offered some and refused, so that's on
you."

"You call the shit that they offered me food?"

"Beggars can't be choosers or however the saying goes."

I pulled a chair away from the table and sat down in it.
Her mouth opened slightly and I saw the mask slip. It took
her no time to put the mask back in place and we were back
where we began.

"Your friend ratted you out. He told us that you were the one
who organized this. Calling him to be your getaway driver and all
of that." Jeremy hadn't said those exact words, but if I could get
her to believe that I knew more than I did, then maybe she'd talk.

Emma rolled her eyes. "I swear no one in this fucking
town can keep their mouths shut."

"He valued his life, seemingly more than you value yours.
I'm sure you'll see each other again eventually and you can
give him a piece of your mind."

I was referring to both of them burning in the depths of
hell, but who knows if she picked up on that. This time,
Emma shook her head and looked down at the table standing
between us. I waited to see if she would speak and was pleas-
antly surprised when she did.

"There're a lot of things you don't understand."

I noticed that she hadn't corrected my assumption.
"Enlighten me then."

"Why does it matter? I'm dead no matter which choice I
make."

She had a good point although I didn't want to kill her. Yet. "What's stopping you from telling me everything you know about what happened with Harlow?"

When she didn't respond, I tried another tactic. "If you tell me who sent you after Harlow, I might think about telling Kingston here to let you go."

I watched as the wheels turned in her head and I could see that she was trying to figure out the best answer that might get her out of this situation alive.

"Falcone did. He funded the whole thing."

That was easier than I thought it would be. "Didn't you tell Harlow you stole that money?" Memories of the night I saved her and the money that she'd hid in the back of her closet resurfaced in my mind.

She glared at me before she responded. "He gave me the money to form a getaway plan with Harlow. I lied and told her that I took it. Now can you let me fucking go? I'm starving."

"I'm not done with questioning you, yet. Why did you target Harlow?"

Emma shrugged. "Because it was easy. It didn't start out that way initially, but Falcone encouraged me after you bought her at the auction. She trusted me enough and Falcone was willing to pay even more money because I had an in with her."

"So initially your relationship with Harlow wasn't influenced by money from Falcone."

Emma nodded and I saw her eyes shift momentarily, the glare fell for just a second and I could see she was slightly hurt by what her relationship with Harlow had become. It was her own damn fault anyway and I had no sympathy for her.

I shared a look with Kingston before looking back at her. My eyes narrowed once more as I took in the despicable human being in front of me.

"If Kingston approves, then I'm sure Cross Sentinel will make some accommodations for better food. But we won't be letting you go."

"Wait, what? You said—"

"I said I'd think about it and I have. I still don't trust you after all the stunts you've pulled."

"But I told you what you wanted to know!"

"You should be happy that I didn't order for you to be killed. Or did it myself."

That got her to be quiet although I could still see the anger growing inside of her. Her rage made me grin. She couldn't be this stupid to think we were going to let her go. Giving her the opportunity to terrorize Harlow again was the last thing on my list. Killing her would have ended any chance of her doing that, but something in my gut told me that now wasn't the right time. She might have some usefulness in the future.

I looked at Kingston again and said, "I'm done with her."

11

ACE

The next afternoon, I found myself sitting at Harlow's bedside, quietly watching television while Harlow slept. I couldn't remember the last time, if ever, I watched this much TV.

With a sigh, I stretched my body out and debated whether it was worth taking a nap myself. Things were quiet and this would be the perfect opportunity to get some shut-eye before my meeting with Parker tonight.

I brushed the hair out of Harlow's face and tucked it behind her ear. She gave me a small smile in her sleep and I couldn't help but return it even though she couldn't see my face. I shook my head at how mushy I was becoming because of her. Without a doubt, I needed to focus on finding Falcone. I mentally started pulling together plans about what I was going to do if he hadn't been found once I brought Harlow home. If he hadn't been located, I was going after him. Sometimes, it was more efficient to do things yourself.

I softly pushed back the chair I was sitting in and stood up. I walked over to the makeshift bed that I'd been sleeping on since Harlow arrived. Before I lay down on the bed, I pushed the blanket out of the way. After a glance to see the time, I put my phone near my head and pulled the blanket up around me. It didn't take long for me to feel myself start to drift off to sleep.

SOMETHING WAS LIGHTLY SHAKING the cushion near my head. I tried to ignore it, but the motion was consistent. I opened my eyes wider when I found my phone screen lit up. At least I'd gotten thirty minutes of sleep.

I bit back a groan as I snatched the phone from its place next to me and picked it up. It was my grandfather.

My eyes found Harlow and saw that she was still resting. I was glad it hadn't woken her up.

I debated with myself whether it was worth answering it and against my better judgment, I whipped the blanket that was on me off and walked out of the room because I didn't want to disturb Harlow.

As soon as I was out of earshot, I answered the phone and said, "Hello?"

"Ace, I want to speak with you."

"You already did at the board meeting."

"There's more I want to discuss and I've even made things easier for you. I'm downstairs."

That comment made me raise an eyebrow. "Downstairs where?"

"Cross Industries Hospital."

Pissed didn't even begin to describe how I felt.

How the hell did he know we were here? I needed to tell

Damien that he wasn't allowed here under any circumstances. Granted, if he was outside of the hospital, I didn't know how much Damien could do about it since I wasn't sure if outside of the hospital was public or private property. Until I could do that, I would deal with this myself.

"Why are you at a hospital?" Playing coy might work to my advantage because I didn't know what he knew and what he didn't.

"Because I heard Harlow had been in a car accident, son."

The gentleness in his voice was something I hadn't heard before. It was foreign to my ears and I didn't know how to feel. I remembered that soon after my mother had died, my grandfather had changed his mind about taking me in and forgot all about mentioning it, saying that he had no time to raise another child.

He was the last thing I wanted to think about during this time, but it looked like I had no choice. I drew a hand across my face and into my hair as I debated my answer. "Fine, but I want to know how you know where I am and why you're here."

"Of course."

"I'll be down in a couple of minutes."

"Okay, bye."

I hung up and walked back into Harlow's room to check on her. She'd moved her head at some point but was still asleep. I grabbed my coat, threw it on before lightly kissing her forehead. I walked out the door and closed it behind me, mentally vowing to be back before she woke up.

When I stepped out of the elevator, I could see him standing just beyond the automatic sliding doors of the hospital. I masked any feelings that I had as I strolled out the doors until I was face to face with the man of the hour.

"Grandfather."

Jerald Bolton stood before me once again, which I must say, was another surprise I hadn't seen coming. Maybe I should have since he could have easily informed me that he was changing the tradition he'd set when he'd retired and would be attending the board meeting in person.

When he turned to face me, I grew suspicious because of the look on his face. There was a level of concern that I'd never seen before. Was he about to drop something else into my lap? Why else would he make another surprise appearance since he's never cared about anything other than himself?

"I came over here as soon as I heard what happened."

I folded my arms over my chest. "What did you hear?"

"That someone you were involved with was involved in a car accident."

"How did you hear about that?" My patience was wearing thin and I was irritated that he'd come here when he hadn't been invited. The last thing I wanted to do was have this conversation so the faster it happened, the happier I'd be.

My grandfather's eyes studied me, probably trying to figure out where I was going with this line of questioning. "From Mayor Henson. He and I are old friends and he mentioned the accident had happened when he found out I was in town for a bit."

That was interesting. I needed to talk to Kingston about what he told the mayor's team to avoid having the police and other emergency personnel involved. Because the whole point of this was to avoid having any news of this getting out and now I was dealing with this.

"Damnit, I forgot something. Let me head to my car and get it."

I didn't say anything as he walked away from me and to his car. He was fortunate enough to have found a parking spot near the entrance of the hospital.

When he walked back toward me, he had some flowers in his hand.

"Flowers?"

"For your lady friend."

I stared at the flowers in his hand as he held them out for me to take. I took them and had already made up my mind about what I was going to do about them.

"Surprised you didn't have a driver bring you here."

"I thought about it, but it would have been quicker for me to drive than wait for someone to come to me and pick me up. How is she doing?"

Suspicion ran through my veins. I had to remind myself it made sense to ask how someone who was in the hospital was doing. I debated with myself how much I wanted to tell him. "She's fine. Doctors are optimistic about her recovery."

"I'm glad to hear it. She seems like a lovely girl."

It wasn't what he said that put me on edge. It was how he said it. "You don't know a thing about her."

"If you're together and you care about her enough to be here with her at the hospital, she obviously means something to you. I trust that she is a good person and treats you well because I trust your judgment."

"That's a first."

"I deserve that."

I didn't disagree with him, but my hatred of him wouldn't get this conversation done quicker.

"Listen, I'll be in town for a couple more days. I know you have your hands full, but if there's anything I can do. Please let me know."

I nodded but said nothing. There was no chance in hell that I'd call him and both he and I knew that.

He patted me on the shoulder and I shook his hand off, glaring at him in return. "See you later, son."

As I watched him drive away, another question popped into my mind that I wished I'd asked when he was standing in front of me. How the hell had he known we were at this hospital since we'd transferred from Brentson Hospital to CIH.

I walked back into the hospital and fished my phone out of my pocket. Three clicks and I was calling Kingston. My patience was wearing thin as I waited for him to pick up the phone. When he did, I came across a garbage can and immediately tossed the flowers into it.

"Yeah?"

I waited until I'd walked into the elevator and the doors shut behind me before I responded. "I want you to tell me everything you told Mayor Henson and find out what you can about my grandfather tracking me and Harlow."

"Mr. Bolton."

I gave a small smile to Thea, Parker's assistant, as she addressed me. She looked to be around what would have been my mother's age and I'd usually seen her when I entered the building for a Chevalier meeting. Her pleasant demeanor didn't fool me. If she worked for Parker Townsend, the chairman of the Chevaliers, who knew what the hell she'd seen or heard.

"Does Parker ever let you go home? It's 7:55 p.m."

"We tend to keep later hours here, so I don't mind. I'll let Mr. Townsend know that you're here."

I nodded and instead of taking a seat in one of the chairs in the waiting room, I decided to look out the window. There was plenty I could do for work on my phone while I waited for Parker, but I didn't want to.

Choosing to do this gave me an opportunity to calm the tension and anger that I felt on the car ride over here. It was directed at how much of a clusterfuck this had become and me having to go to Parker at all for this.

I needed to let that go because there was nothing I could do to change it at this point. I did still trust Cross Sentinel and they were watching over Harlow and Marnie while I was gone. Marnie offered to keep Harlow company this evening and I was hopeful that this would be the last night that she'd be in the hospital anyway. Her doctors seemed optimistic that she'd be released tomorrow and I was more than ready to get her home and into a more comfortable environment.

"Ace."

I turned and found Parker walking toward me; his hand outstretched for me to shake. He stood in front of me with a serious look on his face. I wondered if it was related to me or to something else.

"Parker," I said as I returned the gesture. "I hope this is a productive meeting for both of us."

"I believe it will be. Come, follow me."

I nodded my head at Thea before I did as he said. I followed him through the door and down the short hallway. It was a hallway I had never been in even though I had been to numerous meetings at the headquarters.

There was an awkward silence between us, and I thought it was best to ask the question to fill the quiet.

"Why did you want to meet here?" It wasn't the best icebreaker, but it was all that I could think of. I couldn't help but study his office and I had to admit, it wasn't what I'd expected.

"I was already working here, and it's closer to Cross Industries Hospital."

Of course, he knew about Harlow.

"Do you do most of your business here?"

"Depends on the week. It's helpful to have an office here though, because of my other businesses on the other side of town."

I didn't have to continue the conversation because we walked up to a door. Parker opened the door and allowed me to walk in first before following behind me. Thankfully, the office was already well lit and I took the opportunity to study my surroundings before grabbing a seat.

The office reminded me of the rest of the decor choices at the Chevaliers headquarters. The dark colors and some of the historic memorabilia made me wonder how much Parker had put into personalizing this space. It reminded me of myself in my estate outside of the city before Harlow had entered my life.

"What's up with that?" I said, gesturing to the photo on his desk. It was a photo of Parker holding what appeared to be a sniper rifle.

Before Parker sat down, he reached over and turned over the photo on his desk. "It was a different life."

Interesting. His body language told me it was something he didn't want to talk about and that wasn't the reason why I was here anyway.

"I want all the information you have on Falcone's whereabouts and I'll tell you what happened with Kiki."

"Deal's a deal." Parker leaned forward in his chair and clasped his hands together. "Falcone isn't in Florida anymore, but I do know where he'll be later this week."

"Oh really?" That news was more than welcome and would give us more time than I thought to pull something together. I thought we might have a few hours' notice at most.

"Yes. He's going to be at The Sphynx on Saturday night."

I raised an eyebrow. "Seriously? He has the nerve to come back here and show his face with everyone after him."

"He had a deal that he couldn't refuse."

"Did you have something to do with this 'deal'?"

"No."

I gritted my teeth before relaxing my mouth. "Care to elaborate?"

"I would if I could, but I can't, so here we are."

I shook my head as my irritation began to grow. "How do I know you're not just bullshitting me?"

Parker stared me down, clearly not appreciating that I was challenging him. "I know you probably have doubts crawling up your ass after your girl's accident, so I'm not going to take it personally. But you and I both know that I'm right and you and whoever you're bringing with you need to be at The Sphynx on Saturday night. I've heard the meeting is supposed to be around ten."

The club sounded familiar. I rolled the name around in my mind before I remembered why I knew the name: it was a place that Kiki Hastings was affiliated with.

Fuck.

What were the chances that out of all the places in New York City, he would be attending a function at this establishment? Although it made sense for him not to go back to Bar 53 due to him being hunted, this threw another layer on an already complicated ordeal. To make things worse, it made me wonder if Kiki was attempting to haunt me beyond the grave.

"How'd you find this out?"

"I have my sources. Will you be going? I'll have to make arrangements to get you in."

This was the only lead I had and I knew I had to take it. There might not be another chance and my desire for justice won out over any other feelings I had.

"Fine, I'll be there. I'll tell Kingston."

"Don't worry about that. He should be finding out about it right about... now."

As if he'd triggered the reaction, my phone buzzed, but I didn't dare move. "How the hell—"

"It's best that you don't know."

"And if I want to?"

Parker shrugged. "I'll have to kill you and I don't mean that to be cheesy."

I'd like to see him try. "Can you tell me if it has to do with your position here?"

He nodded once but didn't verbally confirm.

"Now what's the story on Kiki?"

He'd effectively changed the story, but that wasn't enough to make me give him what he wanted yet. "Why does it matter to you what happened to Kiki? I'd figured she'd pissed off enough people that no one would really care that she was no longer walking among the living."

Parker tapped his finger twice on the desk in front of him. "She did and I'm no different. This is more curiosity than anything."

That wasn't a good enough answer. "She's been dead for a while now. Why are you asking questions about her now?"

Parker stared at me but didn't respond. I imagined he was weighing his options about how to answer me. "Someone I used to know had a connection to her and I was curious."

The finality on his face told me that that was all I was going to get out of him and that was good enough for now.

I took a deep breath before I began my story. "I also had a connection to Kiki. A bad one that I don't want to relive. I waited and waited for the perfect time to strike, and then, when the time was right, I burned her alive in a car and enjoyed every second that I heard her screams. She deserved every bit of that."

"I don't doubt that. Thank you for telling me."

"Is that all you wanted to know?"

"Yes. It explains quite a bit for me." He tapped his fingers on the desk again and I knew he was thinking. I took it as my cue to get ready to leave.

"If you don't have anything else to discuss with me, I'm going to leave. I have to call Kingston back and prepare to hunt down Falcone."

Parker was gazing off into a corner of the room and I wondered if he'd heard me or not. A soft cough from me brought him back to the present and he turned to look at me.

"Did you hear what I said?"

"Yeah, you're calling in Kingston for reinforcements so that you have backup when you enter The Sphynx to get Falcone."

It was my turn to nod. "If you hear anything else, call me immediately."

"Of course."

I stood up and turned to leave the room when I heard Parker call my name. I turned to face him, wondering what he'd forgotten to mention.

"Call me if you need me. I'll be there."

"Why?" I was suspicious of his ulterior motives. I was still confused as to why he'd wanted to help me anyway.

"Let's just say I was in your position once and we both know until you kill the fucker, he's going to keep coming after you and hurting what's yours."

13

HARLOW

I pushed the button to roll down the window and sighed. Just doing something as simple as that was enough to make me smile. I allowed myself to lean back on the headrest and close my eyes. It felt so good to be out of the hospital, but I couldn't deny that I was worried about riding in a car again, even though I wasn't driving. That was put to the test when Kingston was forced to slam on the brakes.

My eyes shot open and I clenched the armrest on the door when the SUV came to a screeching halt. Ace grabbed my hand and the gesture made me feel safer immediately. I mumbled reassurances to myself that I wasn't the one driving the vehicle as my heart raced from the events that had just occurred. Ace leaned over and whispered sweet nothings in my ear, and when I looked up at him, he was glaring at Kingston through the rearview mirror.

Kingston held up a hand and said, "Sorry. Someone cut in front of me and I had to brake quickly. Is everyone alright?"

"Are you okay?" Ace asked me. When I confirmed I was, he turned to Kingston and said, "We're fine."

I gripped Ace's hand hard and it felt as if the words that had just left his lips were a lie. I wasn't fine even if I pretended to be. I'd tried to prepare myself for what I thought might have been a hellish ride home due to the accident I'd just experienced and being caught up in my own head.

Thankfully, the ride wasn't too long and soon we were pulling up in front of a large building that seemed familiar, but I couldn't quite place it.

Kingston confirmed that he was going to check out some things before meeting us upstairs, which was fine by both me and Ace. Ace didn't let me take one step into the building. He swooped me up into his arms and carried me over the threshold like I was his bride. I wasn't complaining, but the scene that was being painted wasn't lost on me.

When we walked into the lobby, that was when it all clicked. I recognized the doorman of the building from our brief interaction when Ace brought me with him to see this place. He held the door open with a small smile and I couldn't help but smile back.

"Don't worry about your things in the car. I'll have them delivered in a moment, Mr. Bolton."

"Thanks, Franz."

I was taken aback by Ace's response. When had he found the time to introduce himself to Franz?

Franz helped us to the elevator and once we were safely inside, I looked up at Ace and said, "When did you guys meet?"

"I've been coming here more often since you were in

Cross Industries Hospital. That was the whole purpose of finally buying a place in the city, right?"

He had a point. I just didn't think that someone that truly loved to bask in his grumpiness would go out of his way to make more friends. "Touché and you're right, that makes sense. I thought you would have taken me back to your estate."

Ace looked at me for a second before his eyes focused on the elevator doors. "This was closer and there are a few things I wanted to show you."

When the elevator chimed, announcing that we'd reached the top floor, the elevator opened and Marnie greeted us once we arrived at the front door.

"Welcome home, Harlow."

Her words stunned me, but there was no time to react. I looked up at Ace and found him staring at me. Neither of us said a word before Marnie closed the door behind us and Ace allowed my feet to touch the ground for the first time since we'd left the hospital.

I found myself unable to speak. What stood before me couldn't be real life.

"Should I take your silence to mean that you like it?"

Ace's question couldn't force the words out of my mouth either. I took in everything around me and the word shocked couldn't begin to describe how I felt.

When I first saw this place, it was very bare bones, but now it looked as if someone lived here. The cream, brown and green all meshed well together, making the space appear even larger than I remember it looking when I visited it the first time. Now that it had furniture and art in it, I was truly blown away.

"You did all of this?" The question was a foolish one because, of course he had, but I blamed it on my brain short-circuiting due to the state I was in.

"Yes, I did. It didn't take long to pull all of this together and if there is anything you want to change, we can make arrangements to do that too."

I didn't respond as I took my time walking around the living room area. The living room continued the earthy colors that the rest of the suite had and I couldn't be more thrilled. Images of living here and enjoying the big-screen television that hung over the fireplace flooded my mind. I couldn't wait to settle in here.

It was perfect. There were some small tweaks I would make but other than that it felt like home. Much more than the darkened palace that Ace owned in upstate New York. Here, I felt like I belonged and that feeling almost made me cry.

"There's more I want to show you, but if you're not up for it, we can wait."

I held back the tears and said, "You've got to be kidding. Of course, I want to see it now."

"I had a feeling you'd say that. Come on, but we are going to take our time." He held out his arm for me to grab and together we slowly walked around the suite.

The master bedroom was stunning. "Is this what you wanted to show me? Every inch of this place is immaculate."

Ace shook his head. He ran a hand through his hair and said, "No, what I wanted to show you is the last room in the suite... well, outside of the room that Marnie is staying in while we are here."

This was the first time I'd seen him slightly unsure of

himself. His nervous energy was endearing and made me anxious to find out what he hadn't shown me yet.

We walked out of the master bedroom and found ourselves in front of a closed door. Ace glanced at me out of the corner of his eye before turning the knob and letting me walk into the dark room first. When he turned on the lights in the room, I let out a huge gasp and my hands flew to my mouth.

He'd turned this room into his office... well, our office if I were to assume that the other desk was mine. But that wasn't what took my breath away.

It was the large bookcase that was situated behind my desk. I walked over to it, a little more quickly than I wanted, but it was as if I didn't have control over my body anymore. The bookcase was calling out to me and I needed to examine every inch of it and the books it contained.

"How'd I know you'd go straight for the books?"

I slowly looked over my shoulder, not yet trusting myself to move too quickly. "Because you know me."

"That I do," Ace said as he walked over, joining me in front of the bookshelves. "I knew this would make you happy, so it was a no-brainer to do it. I hope this makes you feel at home here."

"I am happy, but home is wherever you are."

I knew it sounded corny as it left my lips, but I didn't care. My heart was using my lips to speak and I had no control over it. Ace didn't laugh at me or crack a smile. Instead, he leaned down and planted a soft kiss on my lips. It felt wonderful to have his lips on mine again. When our connection naturally broke apart, Ace gently laid his forehead on mine and I couldn't help but smile.

"I want you to do whatever you want here."

"So, if I want to paint all of the walls pink, you'll let me?"

Ace's eyes widened slightly and I held back a giggle. I couldn't tell if he thought I was joking or not.

"If that's what you want."

A snort fell out of my mouth followed by my wincing. I still needed to be mindful of my ribs. Ace's lips twitched for a second before a look of concern crossed his features. I patted his hand, letting him know I was okay.

"I was just joking. I wouldn't do it, but maybe I should just because of your reaction."

"Is that a game you want to play, sweetness? The payback for that would be absolutely amazing."

If his words hadn't sent a tremble through my body, his stare did. The small smile on his lips told me that my attempt to comfort him had worked.

"Let's get you settled and resting. Then we can chat about any redesigning adventures you want to take on, okay?"

"Sounds good to me."

Ace wrapped an arm around me and helped me walk back into the master bedroom before walking into the bathroom.

He turned on the bathroom light and asked, "Are you hungry?"

I thought about it for a moment before I said, "I could eat, but I really want to take a shower."

"You'll do both."

"Will you join me?" The question flew out of my mouth before he had a chance to finish his sentence.

Ace's hand traced a pattern on the back of my shoulder and he nodded. "Let me talk to Marnie and then I'll join you."

With that, he left me in the bathroom to look at myself in the mirror. The bruises had faded a bit, thankfully, and I was starting to look more and more like myself again. More importantly, I was starting to feel like myself again, even though there was still some pain from my sprained arm and bruised ribs but in general, I was feeling better. I promised myself I would still take things easy in order to not further aggravate my injuries and hopefully that meant a lot of time resting and reading, which I had no problem doing.

My gaze shifted when I heard some shuffling in the doorway and my eyes met Ace's through the mirror. I gave him a small smile as he walked up to me and wrapped his arms around me softly from behind. He placed a kiss on the top of my head before unwrapping his arms and walking over to the tub to start the shower.

"Are you sure you don't want to take a bath?"

I turned around and leaned back on the countertop as I considered the option. "That would probably be a better idea, if I'm being honest."

I'd been standing for a while and a bath sounded amazing.

Ace set everything up for the bath as the water filled the tub, I had nothing to do but ease the loose-fitting clothes off of my body. The pants were pretty easy but removing the loose button-down shirt was a bit more difficult. Ace walked over and came to my rescue as he unbuttoned the shirt and slipped the fabric off my shoulders. I was left naked except for my panties and I watched as he drank me in. The way his gaze studied my body made me feel a warmth I hadn't been anticipating.

Ace held out his hand and I accepted his help as he

walked me over to the bath and turned the faucet off. He quickly removed his clothes and got into the tub first before once again offering a helping hand so that I could ease my body into the tub. When I was resting my body against his chest, I finally allowed myself to relax. There wasn't a need to fill the silence with endless conversation. Instead, we enjoyed the silence. I was so relaxed that I closed my eyes and allowed myself to imagine that I was on a tropical island, enjoying the beautiful sunrays and the sparkling water.

A low moan came out of my mouth involuntarily.

"You alright?" Ace's voice broke through the relaxation haze I was in.

"Yes. I was imagining that we were on a deserted island and it was orgasmic."

That made Ace chuckle. "Duly noted."

We fell back into a comfortable silence and before long, I felt Ace begin to wash my body and I had no issue with him taking control here. We wrapped up the bath and once we were both dried off and dressed, I was sitting on the edge of the bed.

I cleared my throat and asked, "Can you brush my hair?"

The look on Ace's face was comical. I'd never seen him look unsure about himself and now here we were. He took the brush out of my hand and ran it through my strands.

As Ace was slowly brushing my hair, a knock on the door snatched both of our attention away from the task at hand. He handed me the brush before walking over to the door and opening it and that was when I heard Marnie's voice.

"Dinner is ready. Also, Kingston just arrived and I set a place for him at the dining room table."

"Perfect. Thanks, Marnie."

I watched as the twinkle in Marnie's eyes grew brighter and when she left the room, Ace turned to me.

"After dinner, Kingston and I have some things we need to discuss."

I waved him off. "Fine. I have no other plans other than getting into bed and going to sleep anyway, so I won't be in the way. That bed looks way too inviting."

14

ACE

I stood up from the couch I'd parked myself on and stretched, determined to knock out any of the kinks that had formed in my body as a result of my being stationary for so long. I was back at the brownstone that Kingston had asked me to meet him at when he brought Emma in for us to have a little chat. That discussion had played a role in leading me to where I was today: waiting to move on Falcone.

If Parker's information was correct, Falcone had dared to come back to the city. If it was true, I knew I only had a limited amount of time to catch him if that were the case.

I wasn't surprised that he couldn't stay away from his home turf. It took years to build the connections and money that he had. Who'd want to give all of that up for long? I knew I wouldn't want to.

"Hey, there is something I meant to ask you as a follow-up to our conversation about my grandfather."

It had been something that was weighing on my mind

and now, while we were waiting for instructions to move, it seemed as good a time as any to ask.

"Go on."

"You told me when you approached Mayor Henson about Cross Sentinel taking over the investigation into Harlow's car accident that you only gave him a brief overview of what happened. That doesn't jibe with my grandfather finding out about what happened. This isn't to say that I don't believe you, but I'm wondering who could have leaked it. It could have been a leak from the small crowd that had gathered at the scene, but I'm a bit wary of that explanation."

Kingston slowly nodded. "I am too and have been racking my brain trying to figure it out myself. It wouldn't be unheard of that someone might have recognized you at the scene. Any one of them could have told Henson, who then could have fed that information to your grandfather. You know people talk."

That seemed like a reasonable explanation, but something about it still didn't sit well with me.

"Has he tried to contact you since?"

"My grandfather?"

Kingston nodded and when he stopped, I shook my head.

"Nope. I haven't heard from him since the evening he showed up at CIH. Don't even know if he's still in the country."

"Well, that isn't the worst thing in the world, is it? Him being gone."

He made an excellent point. I noticed the shift in his expression before the next words flew out of his mouth. "How sure are we that Falcone's there?"

I placed my gun in my holster before looking up at

Kingston. "Parker was positive and that's all we have to go on. Slightly off topic, but you called me almost immediately after Parker told me. Who informed you?"

"I have my sources as well."

I didn't give away that Parker had been able to count down to the exact second when Kingston was going to call. It might lead to a discussion that I wasn't willing to have right now because it would be a waste of time and mental space when we needed to be focusing on killing Falcone.

"Do you know how many people are usually in his entourage?"

"When I visited him at Bar 53, he only had Ian, who would sometimes lead people down to his office and a guard that would stand outside his office door. Now that circumstances have changed, he may have more people, but that's what it was when I saw him last."

Kingston made a noise that sounded like *hmph* but said nothing else.

I grabbed my coat and the way it draped around my body ensured that the gun wasn't visible. From what we'd researched, there wasn't any security that might frisk us so we should have no issue walking in there with our weapons as long as they weren't seen.

"I've had men watching the place and Bar 53 since we talked a few days ago. Nothing suspicious and no signs of Falcone. Wanted to take extra precautions just in case he tried any funny shit."

That made sense and I was happy he had. It was something I would sometimes do for him and it made me long for the days when I wasn't a client and instead, we were working on a joint case together. "Good thinking. I'm just hoping that he's not going to skip out on this altogether."

"Same here."

I ran a hand through my hair as I looked at the layout of The Sphynx. It would be easy to get in through the front door, but we didn't know where Falcone would be, which made things tricky. This was now or never.

"Are you ready?"

Kingston's question hung in the air as I glanced at the other men in the room. Before anyone could answer, the door opened and I couldn't help but shake my head when I saw who'd just walked in.

Gage Cross strolled into the room as if we'd been waiting on him.

"What are you doing here?" I asked as I walked up to him. We greeted each other while I waited for Gage to explain his presence.

"I couldn't miss out on the opportunity to shoot some shit up. It's been a while since I've worked with Kingston and there was no way I was missing out on this."

This time I turned to Kingston. "How come you didn't tell me he was joining us?"

Kingston turned to me and said, "I didn't know because he didn't respond to me."

The lack of communication between us was astounding but would have to be dealt with at another time.

"Kingston gave me a brief overview of what was going on since you decided not to call me and tell me anything about this..."

I heard Kingston mumble under his breath something about that might have been a mistake, but my focus wasn't on him. I didn't come here to get berated or to hash this out in front of anyone else, but I couldn't resist. "You haven't been around much either."

Gage's eyes widened slightly for a second and he nodded. "After tonight is over, we're talking."

"Deal."

Kingston cleared his throat. "Can we wrap up this reunion so that we can head out?"

That forced a chuckle from both Gage and me before the three of us filed out of the brownstone one by one.

Once we were seated in one of Cross Sentinel's many SUVs, Kingston gave us more information about the layout of the land. "Several of my guys are sitting outside in unmarked cars. I also have a couple on the inside, scouting the place to see if and when Falcone arrives."

That was good. We had backup in case things did get hairy. In situations such as this, there was always the risk of something not going the way you planned. While you could try to control and manage what you could, there were too many variables where things could go awry.

My thoughts were interrupted by Kingston receiving a text message that appeared on the vehicle's dashboard.

"Target has arrived."

Kingston read the words out loud and I noticed that the SUV started moving faster, as if Kingston had pressed his foot down harder on the gas. According to the GPS, we were seven minutes away and I thanked the luck we were having because NYC traffic wasn't terrible right now. Now if that same luck would crossover into finding Falcone, I would be forever grateful.

"He came early. Way early," said Gage.

"Yeah, I'm wondering what is up with that."

Although Kingston's attention was focused on driving, I could sense the tension radiating off of him. After all, this was important for him too, not only too close this case, but he'd lost two men as a result of Falcone. I'd be ready for payback too and I suspected the rest of his security team was more than willing to nail Falcone's ass to the wall to avenge the deaths of their fallen brothers.

Kingston looked at me quickly before looking back at the road. "Ace, did you hear anything about a change in plans from Parker?"

"Nope," I said as I pulled out my phone to double-check that I hadn't missed anything. I had no new calls or messages.

"It's possible that he didn't know either."

This time, Gage spoke up. "Is it though? The way Parker operates can be... unconventional at times."

He wasn't wrong about that, but my curiosity got the best of me. "What do you know about the way Parker does business?"

"I know that he sometimes has a stick up his ass."

I rolled my eyes when Gage chuckled at his own comment.

"Okay, okay. But seriously, I don't know much. I assume because of his position with the Chevaliers, he knows a whole bunch more shit than we could have ever dreamed of knowing. Who knows who he has connections to or what secrets he's harboring? I also wouldn't want his job ever."

This time I looked over my shoulder at Gage before I spoke. "Why not?"

"From what I've heard, he doesn't have much of a life and I could see it given that he's running his own business and is the chairman of the Chevaliers. It's not what I would want for myself, especially not now."

I suspected he was referring to wanting to spend more time with his girlfriend, Melissa. Now that I knew what that felt like, I didn't blame him one bit.

We fell into a brief silence and I could feel my heart rate beginning to tick up. The closer we got to The Sphynx, the more the energy in the car increased. I hoped this would end in a quick takedown of Falcone and none of us getting hurt, but you never knew.

When we were about a block away, I looked at Kingston and then at Gage. When I turned to face forward, I finally said, "I want to thank you and the entire Cross Sentinel team for doing all of this to catch this bastard. No matter what goes down tonight, it's important that I tell you how grateful I am."

Gage leaned forward as far as his seat belt would let him and clapped a hand down on my shoulder. "Are you getting soft on us, Ace?"

Kingston snickered and I shook my head. Leave it to Gage to try to lighten up the mood, but I was serious about my comment. I was thankful for these two men and the backup team we had behind us. Going at this alone would have been extremely hard, especially with Harlow's state while she was in the hospital.

"No, I'm just trying to get better at showing my appreciation, that's all."

Gage gave me a small smile before sitting back in his seat. "I'm messing with you. Now let's get this asshole."

Kingston held up his hand before he said, "Since we are only a block away, I wanted to mention that my plan was to drag him out of The Sphynx and take him to one of Cross

Sentinel's other properties. Does anyone have an issue with that?"

Both Gage and I shook our heads and about a minute later, Kingston was parking a couple of blocks away from The Sphynx. Together, the three of us strolled up to the club and once it was verified that we were on the VIP guest list, we walked in.

The establishment was like your typical club, nothing too fancy. Had this place also looked like this when Kiki Hastings was affiliated with it?

Fuck.

Where had that come from?

I tried to put the memories that I had with her back in the mental chest that I kept under lock and key because this was not the time. All I wanted to do was stop thinking about her, yet at random times she still entered my consciousness.

It was becoming more and more problematic. Or hell, maybe it always was and I was just starting to realize that. Taking a deep dive into that would have to be saved for another time.

"Do we know where Falcone is right now?"

I found Kingston scanning his phone as he stood next to Gage. "Give me one second."

That second came and left and Kingston still hadn't mentioned Falcone's location. That second turned into a minute and I found myself growing more and more impatient. Every second we wasted was another opportunity for Falcone to go in and get whatever he wanted and then leave. That minute turned into two and I found myself growing more and more impatient. Every second we wasted was another opportunity for Falcone to come in and get whatever he wanted and then leave.

"Do we even know why Falcone is here?"

Gage's question was a valid one. And I hadn't cared so much as to why he was there versus him actually being here.

"Nope. Parker didn't mention the purpose of the meeting other than it was something Falcone couldn't get out of. The only important thing was that we knew where he was going to be."

"Yeah, I don't know either. My source only gave me a time and date, nothing else."

I was still willing to bet that Parker more than likely knew why he was coming here and who he might have been meeting with. I didn't think the answer to that question would get us any closer to finding Falcone than we were right now.

"Aha."

I couldn't remember the last time I heard someone make that noise, but if I was in a different situation I might've laughed because it sounded hilarious coming from Kingston. "I hope this means you know where he is."

The longer we stood around looking as if we didn't have anything to do, the more we probably stood out and that could be problematic depending on who was watching. In a place like this, someone is always watching.

"Yes. He and three members of his entourage are in one of the VIP rooms in the basement. Looks like it's room number four. The stairs leading down to it should be over..." Kingston's voice trailed off as his eyes scanned the room. He didn't make an obvious show as to what he was doing in order to not blow our cover. "It's over there. Your nine o'clock."

I followed his directions with my eyes as I, too, found the staircase leading to the basement. We might be outnumbered but I thought we could handle it. "Is there a way for him to get out of the basement through another exit?"

"There is and I have people on guard ready to stop him if he does make a run for it."

I nodded as I liked what I was hearing. "Does being on the VIP list get us access to the rooms downstairs?"

Kingston gave me a small smile. "Yes, it does and we should move fast now. We are only sure that Falcone brought three other people in his entourage, but we aren't sure if he stationed people in here like we did. Would be easy to do."

It would, which was why we didn't need to waste any more time talking about it. We needed to take action now.

I gestured to the door slightly with my head before I started making my way over to it. Although I kept my face neutral, the thundering of my heart as it pounded in my chest was distracting. I hadn't even felt this when I killed Kiki.

There she was again. Filtering into my mind when I wanted nothing to do with her.

By the time I reached the stairs, I had successfully pushed her to the furthest corner of my mind and began my descent. Out of the corner of my eye, I could see Kingston and Gage following me down the stairs.

It didn't take long to find room number four.

What was weird about it was that there was no one standing outside of the door.

I leaned over to whisper to Kingston. "I don't like this. There's usually someone standing outside his office door and the fact that he hasn't done this in a location that's probably more accessible than his own restaurant doesn't sit well with me."

"I agree. We need to get in there right now."

Without thinking about it for another second, I knocked before opening the door. A woman's gasp greeted us in return. It seemed as if we caught her getting dressed. I swore.

Kingston approached the woman and asked, "What are you doing here?"

"Who the fuck are you?" she asked in return.

Nothing I hated right now more than someone answering a question with a question. I glanced over and saw that Gage had walked into the room before turning my attention back to the woman in front of us. "Who we are isn't important and while Kingston here was being nice, I won't be. I couldn't care less about who you are and I want to know who you were here with."

She rolled her eyes and said, "I was called in to fuck someone. I took over a friend's shift and was told I would make good money doing this job, but he and his friends ran out of here like their asses were on fire."

"You've got to be kidding me," I mumbled. "Which way did they go?"

"This way."

This time it was Gage that answered and all heads swiveled toward him. He'd found a door that had been hidden by the fabric in his hand.

"Yeah, he went—"

I heard nothing else from the woman that we'd found because my attention was zeroed in on the door. Gage opened it and I sprinted down the darkish hallway before he could fully step back. Thankfully, it was still dimly lit enough for me to see or I'd have to slow down to grab my phone or risk hitting something that would tremendously slow my progress. I could hear Gage and Kingston behind me, so I knew they were keeping up with the pace I'd set.

The hall was long, but before long, I found another door that I opened. I pulled out my gun once more and threw the door open, hoping to surprise anyone that might have been on the other side of it. But there was no one.

Instead, it opened into a stairway. I didn't wait for Gage or Kingston as I darted up the first flight of stairs and opened that door. What greeted me on the other side was a wide-eyed woman with a hand covering her mouth in the middle of another hallway. It was clear I'd frightened her, but I didn't have time to rectify that situation.

"Did four men come through here?"

She only nodded and pointed to a door to her left. Without giving her a second glance, I ran to that door and opened it.

If I wouldn't have caused a scene, I would have shouted in disgust. The fact that I was outside on a dark street instead of shooting a bullet into Falcone's head was enough to make me rage.

I glanced at Gage and Kingston as they approached me and said, "That son of a bitch."

Falcone must have left through the same secret passageway we did. Had someone warned him that we were coming?

A few more cuss words flew out of my mouth. My anger made me toy with the idea of blowing The Sphynx up, but it would be a waste of time and still wouldn't bring me a step closer to getting my hands on Falcone.

None of this mattered now because the fucker was still in the wind and we had no way of finding out where he would appear next.

15

HARLOW

I'd reread the same line in this book a million times, or so it felt like, as I waited for Ace to return. He'd told me that he was going to find Falcone and put an end to all of this, but that was all I knew. Maybe it was best I didn't know the details about what was supposed to go down tonight, but I couldn't help but worry about him. I'd hoped that the solution we both wanted would be the one that would come about.

Those thoughts didn't make my nerves any better, however.

Reading usually took my mind away from my reality, but I couldn't seem to focus. It was why I'd reread the same line again before I closed the book and put it on my bedside table next to the lamp that was currently the only light in the room.

Would television help? Probably not because it still gave me the opportunity to think too much.

With a sigh, I snuggled deep into the covers and turned the lamp off. Forcing myself into darkness would probably do little to turn off my brain, but it was worth a shot.

I closed my eyes, and it took a while before I felt my body start to doze off. Before I could get into a deep sleep, I heard what I thought was the bedroom door quietly open. My eyes shot open and when I saw a light appear from around the open door, it confirmed my suspicions.

"Ace?" My question came out as more of a whisper, but it got the job done. I relaxed when he responded.

"I didn't expect you to be awake. It's almost two a.m."

"There was no way I was going to be able to sleep with you out there doing who knows what." I sat up in bed and turned on the lamp, illuminating the room once more. "Is he dead?"

I studied the way that Ace looked and knew that I had answered my own question. The dejection on his face painted a perfect picture. It was clear things hadn't gone the way he'd planned but I still wanted to hear the words out of Ace's mouth.

"We didn't catch him. That slimy son of a bitch escaped and now who knows where he is. If he's smart, which I doubt that he is, he will have gotten out of town quickly." Ace walked over to my side of the bed and sat down on the edge. "I'm keeping my promise to you. He's going to pay for all the pain that he put you through, if it's the last thing that I do."

"Well, I, for one, hope that it's not the last thing that you do."

That caused a small smirk to form on his lips. I couldn't help but smile as well because it was because of me that his mood lightened even temporarily. And I felt more at ease because he was home safe.

"I'm going to take a shower. I want to wash this grime off me. "

"I wish I could join you."

"There's nothing stopping you."

I gave him a sad smile this time. "I should still take it easy."

The look in his eyes told me that he knew I was right. But they also told me they wished I wasn't.

I, too, longed for the time that we used to spend together, bringing us both pleasure in different ways and now we were relegated to this for the time being. It would be worth it in the end, but since I was starting to feel better, the more my mind drifted to the fun we used to have.

Ace gave me a small pat on the knee before he stood up. He leaned down and gave me a delicate kiss on the lips before he walked into the bathroom. After a brief debate with myself, I settled on a solution once I heard the shower turn on. I got out of bed and I ended up standing outside the bathroom door.

Before I could talk myself out of it, I turned the doorknob and pushed the door open a crack. When I didn't notice anything out of the ordinary, I opened the door farther and slid my body through the opening. Although I winced slightly due to my sore ribs, I still was able to close the door behind me silently.

It wasn't like he could hear me over the shower anyway. But that didn't stop me from hearing the grunt that left his lips. My eyes took their time moving down his body and I took my time studying every inch of him. His head was down and I assumed his eyes were closed because he hadn't turned in my direction as if he'd seen me.

The way the water danced across his muscles, showcasing them even more prominently in the bathroom light, made me lick my lips involuntarily. I wanted to do nothing more than to run my fingers along his skin. When I heard a groan come from him, my eyes widened. That was when I figured out what he was doing.

I noticed that one of his hands was on his cock, slowly moving up and down its length. Any thought that I had in my mind as I'd snuck in here had completely flown out the window at the sight of him jerking himself off. His motions grew quicker and I was caught in a trance, watching his hand move up and down, up and down. When he released another moan, it sent a shiver down my spine.

This might have been one of the most erotic things I'd ever seen. And I didn't blame him for needing this release tonight after what he'd been through. A chapter we'd both thought would be closed tonight had been ripped open even more and the stress of it all was intensified.

But what I hadn't realized was that I'd also needed to see Ace like this. Following his motions as the pressure built up inside of him seemed like a treat I didn't deserve. I watched on with anticipation and although I thought I knew how this would end; I couldn't take my eyes off of the scene in front of me.

His pace quickened again and I held back a sigh of my own, on the off chance that he might have been able to hear me. I didn't want to disturb the pleasure that this man of mine was bringing himself.

Mine.

He was mine and I was his. There was no doubt in my mind about that. His love for me shined through daily and I don't know what my life would be like without him in it. That was a lie. I knew my life would feel unfulfilled. Even with the toxic way we met and came together or the danger we'd faced, I still wouldn't trade him in for anything in the world.

A low groan left Ace's lips that turned into a slightly louder growl as he exploded. I wished it had been me bringing him to completion. I bit my lip as I watched him. My body was glued to this spot. At least it was until I remembered that he'd found his release and now I needed to figure out how I was going to sneak back out.

He turned and looked at me over his shoulder. "Like what you see?"

If he hadn't known I was already there, then I knew my gasp could be heard over the water cascading out of the showerhead.

Ace's smirk would be my undoing. "You should have known better than to try to sneak up on me."

"I didn't mean to—"

"Yes, you did and that's completely fine. In fact, I enjoyed it more knowing that you were watching me."

He held out his hand and without hesitation, I took it, not caring where it might lead to. Soon, I found myself being pulled into the shower and once again, a gasp left my lips. He'd made sure not to pull me in fully to avoid getting my left arm wet, but the rest of me was soaked from head to toe.

The smirk on his face turned into a genuine smile as he brushed back some of the wet hair from my face. I refused to fight my own grin. at least, until I watched his lips descended toward mine. Any hints of a smile left my face as my eyes drifted closed and when our lips touched, it felt as if the disappointment from today had never happened.

16

HARLOW

A COUPLE OF WEEKS LATER

Every day, I would come up to the mirror in our bedroom and stare at the progress my body was making toward healing itself. I pulled out my hair tie and let my hair flow into waves around my shoulders. It took a couple of minutes of fluffing and shaking my hair out before I got it to resemble something that could be described as messy waves. The bruises on my face had faded and my ribs were almost as good as new. My sprained wrist was doing much better, although I still tried to stay off of it as much as I could to give it the opportunity to continue healing.

I pretty much felt like my normal self and I would be happy if it weren't for me having to address Ace's mood swings.

It didn't take a rocket scientist to see that Ace had been frustrated beyond belief. His entire mood had changed over the course of the last several days and I knew it was a result of the frustration he felt over not being able to find Falcone. The first week or so, he'd remained his usual self, not portraying much emotion, but I assumed it was eating at him that

Falcone was still at large. By week two, things were starting to shift and it was clear that Falcone's disappearance was weighing on him. While he wasn't an asshole to me, I could see a change in attitude with the people around us as clear as day.

Where he'd been mostly neutral with the people in our lives, snappiness was interjected, fostering a negative environment. I could see that Marnie was walking on eggshells around Ace when they both were in the same room as one another. It wasn't fair to anyone and it needed to end.

I took one final look at myself and realized that this was the best that it was going to get. The white button-down shirt and navy pajama shorts looked somewhat silly together, but I couldn't be bothered enough to change the clothes I'd been lounging in most of the day.

I walked out of my bedroom and into the living room, where I found Ace staring at his computer. Based on the look on his face, it was a wonder that he hadn't tossed the thing in the trash, given how much anger it was obviously causing him.

I looked at the clock and found that it was seven thirty p.m. and if it was work that was causing that look on his face, it was long past quitting time.

"Ahem."

I waited for him to look up at me when I cleared my throat, but he didn't. I repeated myself, this time louder, in hopes of getting his attention, but failed.

With a shake of my head, I walked over to where he was sitting and lowered the screen of his laptop slightly. It wasn't enough to put the laptop into sleep mode, but it did force him to pay attention to me.

The irritation was clear in his dark eyes, but I didn't give a damn.

"I want to talk to you," I said before crossing my arms.

"I'm still working."

I gritted my teeth to keep from rolling my eyes. "Unless what you're doing is absolutely pressing, I think it can wait until tomorrow."

"Oh really? Is that so?"

I could hear the danger in his voice. It reminded me of when I challenged him soon after the auction and I wondered if I'd crossed a line right now that I shouldn't have. Well, it was too late to take it back now.

"I understand that you're pissed about Falcone and not being able to find him, but can you not take it out on the people around you?"

Ace raised an eyebrow and I saw a hint of a smile on his lips. He moved his laptop off his lap before crossing his arms. "Are you trying to boss me around?"

The way he said it caused me to shiver slightly. "It's my job to call you out on your bullshit because no one else will."

"Who gave you this supposed 'job'?"

"You did, whether you know it or not."

I loved our banter because it kept things interesting between the two of us.

"I don't remember agreeing to this."

"You did when you told me you love me."

"Don't remember saying that either."

It was my turn to smirk now. "Well, it seems I need to remind you."

I walked over to him with all of the confidence in the world. There were no doubts that I belonged here, with him, right now. I tossed my leg over his lap and sat down. Our gazes clashed because it was a playful battle of wills to see who would blink first.

It was no secret that he was letting me take control right now. It would take nothing for him to shift the balance, but I appreciated him letting me take control even though that was normally not the case.

"There's something I need to tell you," I said.

"And what's that?"

"We haven't christened the couch yet."

This time, the smile was gone. Seriousness had taken over, which was to be expected.

"Harlow, you're still trying to heal."

"I know that. But I'm also ready for some fun too. I miss us and it's not like I'll be swinging from the chandelier in the dining room."

"Yet."

I couldn't help but giggle at that. The light returned in his eyes when he shifted my body and I slowly moved toward him. I was nervous about whether my body would hurt depending on our positions, but so far, so good. When our lips touched, some of the nervousness I had left my mind and the only thing I was concerned about was how long it would take to get his cock inside of me.

When I moaned, Ace took the opportunity to slip his tongue inside of my mouth, causing our tongues to dance as we fought over who was in control. His hands weaved their way into my hair and the difference between that and a kiss was obvious. It felt as if he was trying to hold back but it was a losing battle.

When our kiss broke naturally, he pulled my hair to his

left, giving him better access to my neck, which I thought he would have no problem taking advantage of. Instead, his fingers ran along my throat as if he were studying it and me.

His stare burned a hole through me that warmed me from the inside out. I'd never felt a passion this bright with someone and I hoped it would never end.

When his lips tickled my neck, I sighed in contentment, happy to have him touching me again. His fingertips rested on my thighs, the perfect anchor for the fun we were sure to have.

He gave my neck another kiss and a nibble before he pulled back and said, "Unbutton the shirt."

My hands hovered in the air for a moment before I did as he said. His eyes watched my every move as if committing it to memory so that he could run the scene over again and again in his mind. I stared at him as I unbuttoned the buttons, one by one and his eyes never moved from my chest. It was as if he thought if he moved his eyes away, I would disappear.

But I never planned on leaving him again and I could feel that he felt the same.

I wiggled my shoulders a bit and the white shirt slipped but was still wrapped around my chest, covering my breasts from his eyes. Without saying a word, he took the fabric into his hands and pushed it away from my body, leaving me naked from the waist up. My nipples hardened as soon as they felt the cool air.

"You don't know how hard it's been to not have you in every way imaginable."

"I could say the same about you."

Ace didn't say another word. Instead, he palmed my

breast before sticking a nipple into his mouth. My head fell back as he teased my nipple with his tongue. The desire I had for him increased tenfold when he used his other finger to pinch my nipple. I cried out in ecstasy before I brought my head back up and looked at Ace. His eyes found mine immediately.

"You liked that, huh? Good to know," he said against my breast. He nibbled on the side of my breast before moving onto my other nipple.

"Um—" I stopped myself from speaking because whatever I was trying to say had left my mind. It was probably better that way if I was being honest.

My body took on a mind of its own as I found myself moving my body against his while on his lap. I could feel his cock hardening under my ass. It took everything in me to not stand up, remove his dick from his pants and watch as his eyes rolled back while I gave something only I could give.

Instead, I felt Ace lift me up slightly before he maneuvered our bodies so that I lay with my back on the couch. My heart slammed in my chest with anticipation as I waited to see what he would do next. His hands went to my hips and discarded my panties and shorts in one sweeping motion.

He yanked the sweater he'd had on over his head and soon his pants and boxer briefs followed. I was left staring at his perfect form until he decided that no more time would be wasted and he climbed back on the couch.

When his body was hovering over me, he moved his hand and touched my pussy. He decided that the best course of action was to continue to tease me instead.

I growled, surprising both me and him.

"What do you want, sweetness?"

"You. I fucking want you."

"But do you want my fingers, my cock, or my mouth?"

I gritted my teeth. His teasing was going to be the end of me. "I want your cock because it's been too long."

"Good answer," he said before sticking his finger in me. This time, it was his turn to groan. "You're so fucking wet for me, baby. Widen your legs for me."

I bit my lip as I followed his instructions. His body fit between my legs perfectly and I felt the head of his cock teasing my pussy as he moved it up and down my pussy lips.

"Ace." His name came out like a warning from my mouth. If he didn't do what we both wanted him to do, then I would—

That thought was unnecessary because he sank himself into my heat.

"Holy shit. This feels incredible." The words left my mouth in a jumbled mess and I wasn't even sure if Ace understood what I said. He didn't ask for clarification, so either he had or was preoccupied with the task at hand.

Ace slowly slid his cock inside of my body, inch by inch. When he was fully buried in me, he did the same thing over and over again. I could tell that he was doing this because of my injuries. The way he took his time with me wasn't like anything we'd ever done. I loved when we attacked each other like animals, acting on pure instinct as we tried to give the other what they needed. But this time was different. It was more emotional than I'd expected it to be and it was easy to see why.

"Faster," I said as I closed my legs around his waist.

"Are you sure?"

All I did was nod, not trusting myself to say the proper words.

"What's the magic word?"

If I didn't want him to fuck my brains out, I would have rolled my eyes. "Please."

"Good girl."

I didn't have the opportunity to respond because he robbed me, once again, of any thoughts when his pace quickened. I knew I was just along for the ride.

Our bodies moved completely in sync as if we were made for each other. And I knew it was because we were. The sound of our bodies making each other deliriously happy was enough to make me cry.

"I'm so close." My words came out in short spurts. It was as if I was running a marathon, and in a way, it symbolized our entire relationship. We started out fast and hard, but when it came to building something long lasting, slow and steady would help us in the long term.

"Fuck, baby," Ace said as he pumped into me.

His hand squeezed my breast before making its way down to where we were connected. He flicked his hand over my clit and my pleasure grew to an astronomical level. I grabbed one of the pillows on the couch and used it to cover my face, but that didn't last long.

The pillow was ripped from my grasp, and I found a wild look in Ace's eyes. "You aren't going to deny me your screams of pleasure. I want to hear you calling my name, begging me to let you come."

"Please, Ace. I want to come so bad." And I meant every word.

His tempo increased, and soon I found myself screaming

as I came all over his cock. But he didn't stop there. No, he needed to find his release too.

When he followed my orgasm with one of his own, his grunts turned into a deep roar that I'd never heard him do before. The animalistic nature of all of this wasn't lost on me.

Ace slowed his pace down as we both tried to catch our breath. When he removed himself from me, an ache replaced him and I wished he hadn't moved.

Another minute passed before he picked me up and carried me into the bedroom just before he went into the bathroom to grab what I assumed would be a washcloth. When he reappeared with said washcloth in hand, I couldn't help but smile as he came over to me and made sure to clean the both of us up. He tucked me into bed and soon joined me by pulling me into his arms.

I don't know how long we stayed like that, but when his phone rang on his bedside table, I jumped slightly because I hadn't been expecting the loud, intrusive noise to pierce through the bubble we'd created.

"I need to take this."

"Why?"

"Parker is calling me and I need to take it."

"Fine. Although I'm shocked you'd want to go anywhere, given the current state of affairs." I gestured to my naked body and gave him a knowing smirk.

"You'll pay for that."

I shrugged. "I know."

When he left the room, I found it harder and harder to keep my eyes open. My body began to give in to the urge to sleep.

I must have dozed off for a bit, but I was still conscious

enough to hear the bedroom door open. However, I couldn't find the strength to open my eyes until I felt a dip in the bed when Ace sat beside me.

"Sweetness."

"Yes?" My voice was nothing more than a whisper.

"I'm going to need to head out."

That forced my eyes open as if someone had poured ice-cold water on me. I sat up and pulled the sheet around me. "Wait, why?"

"Falcone has been found."

17

ACE

"How'd you find him?"

Kingston and I were sitting in his SUV. I'd entered the vehicle only a few seconds after parking my car a few blocks away.

Kingston rubbed a hand along the back of his neck. "You'll never guess."

"Try me."

"He showed up at Bar 53. My guys were still on the spot, so I say we go in and fuck some shit up. Gage was pissed about not being able to shoot shit up last time so he said he would meet us there."

I couldn't help but smirk. Of course, he wanted to shoot shit up.

"There's no way he's getting out of this. This will end tonight, I promise you."

"Good, because I made a promise to my girl to end this and I'm tired of prolonging the inevitable."

Kingston tilted his head and said, "There's Gage. We'll have a short debriefing before going in."

"Got it."

We waited for Gage to get into the back seat of the SUV and he spoke first. "The gang's all here."

"If we have to do any more get-togethers ever again, I would prefer they be over drinks instead of dead bodies."

That forced a chuckle from Gage, and even I had to smirk at my own joke. Although sometimes I didn't like to admit it, I did cherish these guys. Gage and I'd both had run-ins with Kiki, me more so than him because he had a loving family to put an end to it in his corner. And I hadn't.

Did I have some resentment about it now? Not so much, but I did when I first found out about Gage's experience with Kiki. It was foolish of me to be angry about it because at least someone else had been spared the pain that I'd felt, but I wished that someone had also done the same for me.

I shifted my thoughts about Kiki to the side and turned to Kingston in the driver's seat. He gave us a rundown about what they found out about Bar 53 and how we should approach entrances and exits, how many people we suspected there to be in the restaurant, etc. Our aim was only to hurt Falcone and any of his minions but there could be innocent bystanders that we wanted to avoid if possible.

Cross Sentinel would once again be providing backup, but we would be taking the lead. That was fine by me.

Deep in my bones, I could feel that this was the end. "I'm willing to bet money that Falcone is in his office. It's downstairs in the basement."

"Then we should go around the back. There's a door that should lead to a flight of stairs that will take us into the basement. I'll let my guys know they are going in through the front."

I checked my gun and said, "You lead, and then I'll take over once we're inside."

"That works for me," Gage chimed in.

Kingston nodded, acknowledging that he understood the plan and before I knew it, we were taking the long way around toward the back of Bar 53.

The dark alleyway was about as dingy as I expected. The cigarette butts on the ground told me that many of Bar 53's employees took their breaks out here. We looked around and found no obvious cameras near the back door. Kingston crept up to the door, checked to make sure it was locked before proceeding to unlock it. He peered into the building, gun drawn in case someone was near this door. Once we knew the coast was clear, the three of us slipped inside and quickly scanned the room for any immediate threats.

I walked around Kingston and led the group down a hall before we came to a point where we needed to go left or right. It didn't take long for me to decide because almost as soon as I saw the guard that usually stood outside of Falcone's door, a loud bang occurred upstairs. I knew it had to be Cross Sentinel breaching the top floor. We needed to move quickly because now Falcone and his guard were alerted that something was amok upstairs.

Before anyone else could do anything, I raised my gun and shot at the man guarding Falcone's door before he could spot me. He immediately cried out and went down. I sprinted to the door and opened it, not bothering to check to see if he was dead.

Falcone was sitting behind his desk, eyes wide and mouth agape. The startled look in Falcone's eyes when I entered would stay with me for the rest of my life. I enjoyed making him squirm, and the look of pure fright on his face was more than worth it.

"Did you think you could waltz back into New York City without me knowing? You were better off continuing to hide under whatever rock you crawled under."

Falcone didn't respond, instead choosing to stare me down as if I hadn't said a word, so I continued.

"Hands on your desk. I don't want you trying any funny shit like pressing any buttons that might set off a silent alarm."

He didn't move at first and when I gestured to my gun, he placed his hands on the flat surface. Another loud boom went off and I glanced at Gage and Kingston for a second.

"Why don't you two go upstairs and see what they are up to? I can handle this piece of shit by myself."

"Are you sure?" Gage asked the question.

"Positive."

"Come on," Kingston said to Gage, and I heard when they left the room.

"Stand up," I said as I looked at the pathetic man before me. This time he didn't hesitate and stood up. I ate up the distance between us and threw a punch before he could blink. His head jerked back due to the force from the hit. I couldn't resist and hit him again before sticking the muzzle of my gun under his chin.

"You tried to have someone come after Harlow again."

Falcone looked at me with a puzzled expression on his face. "I don't know what the hell you're talking about. I didn't send anyone after your girl."

"Fucking liar," I said as another one of my punches landed

on his face. Letting my rage out felt wonderful. Most would say it wouldn't solve anything, but I didn't listen to most people. "Lying to me isn't going to save you now because it's either I kill you or I can call Will, and he can continue to torture you instead."

"I'm. Not. Lying."

I narrowed my eyes at him and said, "Are you telling me you didn't send Ian after Harlow? Nor did you give Emma the means to set up Harlow or try to kidnap her?"

"I let Ian do what he wanted on his own time and I couldn't help that he was infatuated with Harlow."

That made me see red. "To the point where he attacked her twice? And I know you fucking knew about the first time because that was how she got involved in the auction to begin with."

Falcone shrugged. "Turned into a good thing for the both of you, didn't it? You got a bitch and she can now spend all of your money how she sees fit."

My expression remained passive and I suspected Falcone thought I was going to punch him again. Wrong.

I took my gun and shot him in his left hand. His howling was music to my ears. Watching him scream out in pain due to one of my brilliant ideas was an achievement, if I do say so myself.

"That looks painful," I said as I gestured to Falcone's hand.

"You fucking think!"

"Wouldn't have happened if you told the truth," I said. It was a lie because I had every intention of killing him tonight but torturing him was an added bonus. "Now if you tell me the truth, I'll think about sparing your life."

"Can I grab that towel over there to wrap it around my wound?"

I glanced over to where he gestured. "If it'll make you feel any better."

Falcone moved as quickly as he could and wrapped the dark towel around his bleeding hand. Another loud bang occurred and his eyes shot to the ceiling.

"It's all over now. Now tell the truth. Why did you mess with Harlow?"

With a sigh, Falcone finally said, "It was a way to reward Ian for being a good employee."

"Harlow did absolutely nothing to you outside of her owing you money and you had no problem tossing her aside like a piece of meat to Ian. Then you sold her off in order to pay her debt and then some. Anything to make a dollar is all you gave a shit about."

His eyes refused to meet mine, confirming the details I'd drawn together. "You're a sick fuck, you know that?"

My words forced him to snap his head in my direction. "I'm the sick fuck? You're the one who spent a million dollars on her."

His opinion of me meant nothing and I'd been called worst. In fact, his little dig made me smile. "How was Emma connected to this? Why did she work for you when she didn't owe you any money?"

The shocked look and the lack of words from Falcone told me that he was surprised that I knew that information. He winced and looked down at his towel-covered hand before looking back at me. "I used Emma as a way to spy on my other employees. By paying her under the table, it allowed me to gain information about anyone because while they didn't trust Ian, they'd trust her."

"And her setting up Harlow and then trying to orchestrate an attempt to kidnap her?"

This time Falcone shook his head. "I haven't seen Emma since she stole thousands of dollars from me. And if I do find that thieving bitch..."

I didn't trust Falcone, but if what he was saying was true, then we had a problem. When Falcone thought his admission might have been enough to distract me, he attempted to make a run for it. When he thought he'd just made it past me, I raised my gun and aimed down. Instead of attempting to block his exit, I shot him in the foot and he crumpled to the ground in a pile of limbs.

"Don't be an idiot."

His moans on the floor did little to mask the cough that came from the door. I did a one-eighty and found Kingston and Gage standing in the doorway.

"Upstairs is clear," Gage said.

"Good," I replied before bending down to look at Falcone's face withered in pain. It brought me an immense amount of pleasure to see him like this.

"Kingston?"

My voice brought everything to a standstill in the room, including Falcone's groans. All eyes were focused on me. Good. That was where they should be. "Call Will and tell him he can come and pick up Falcone's remains. He can thank me later. Oh, and by the way, if he doesn't mind, I would like a photo of Falcone's head on a silver platter."

Falcone's eyes widened until they were as big as flying saucers.

"No, but you said—"

"I know what I said, and I decided to go with plan *B*."

When his eyes widened as I raised my gun a final time, I hoped the image of the smirk on my face would be imprinted in his mind as he burned in hell for eternity. I pulled the trigger and watched as the man before me immediately collapsed, ending his struggle. I walked over to Gage and Kingston. Gage handed me a towel, and I wiped my hands off. A shower would be needed as soon as I got home.

My eyes shifted between Kingston and Gage before I said, "Falcone didn't take responsibility for Harlow's accident, so either he's lying or—"

"Someone else made the call," Kingston finished my sentence with a grim look on his face.

"I had no problem taking Falcone out and let's be real, the world is a better place without him in it, but it could mean that we are looking for someone else. But that is a thought for tomorrow because I'm going home." I started walking out of Falcone's office.

"Hey Ace?"

I stopped and turned to look at Kingston.

"We might have a lead on the special project you wanted me to work on."

I ran through all of the possible things that he could have been talking about in my mind, but it took a second for me to remember. I contributed my slight delay to still feeding off of the high from killing Falcone. "Harlow's—"

I cut my response short because Kingston nodded his head. This was the best news that I could have heard after such a thrilling evening.

"Okay, send me what you have when you get a chance, but more importantly, get some rest."

Kingston chuckled before he said, "Aww, Ace, I didn't think you cared."

Gage's smile could light the entire room and I fought the urge to roll my eyes at the both of them.

I shrugged. "It happens sometimes, but let's keep it between the three of us."

18

HARLOW

I paced past my bed for what felt like the billionth time as I waited to hear back from Ace. When this happened a couple of weeks back, I thought I was nervous, but nothing compared to how I felt now. The last time that Ace went after Falcone felt like a false alarm and this time felt like the real thing.

I rubbed my right hand down my thigh as I walked to the other side of my room. I was still trying to make sure that I didn't put too much pressure on my wrist even though I hoped to remove the bandage on it in a couple of days because it felt so much better.

Ace had my full support and I couldn't wait to be back in his arms, but I couldn't deny that the sinking feeling that he might get hurt or killed lay in the back of my mind. I'd already called down to the doorman about thirty minutes ago to see if he'd seen or heard anything from Ace, and he confirmed he hadn't. It seemed like a better option than talking to the man that was currently guarding my front door until Ace came home.

I yanked open the bedroom door and walked into the kitchen. Grabbing a glass of wine might be the perfect way to distract myself and calm my nerves because not even reading a book had worked to take my mind off the events I assumed were occurring tonight. Should I be drinking this late? No. But was I going to? Yes.

I poured myself a glass and lifted the vessel to my mouth. I took a larger gulp than normal, but I didn't care. With my glass in hand, I walked over to my couch and sat down as memories of the time we spent here, just a few short hours before, rose to the surface. I couldn't help but smile to myself.

I drank from my glass again, this time choosing to sip instead of taking a large gulp. As I was putting the glass down, I heard something at the front door that made the hairs on the back of my neck stand up. Instead of placing the glass on the coffee table in front of me, I clenched it, hoping it wouldn't break in my hand, all the while thinking I might be able to use it as a weapon if the need arose.

But there was no need for me to panic because as soon as the front door opened, my eyes met Ace's.

The air around him was different this time. There was an ease surrounding him that hadn't been around him before and that made me almost giddy. If it was because of what I hoped, that meant I was free. Free to live the life I wanted without having to worry about whether someone was in the wings, ready to kill me.

"He's dead," I said confidently.

"He is."

A rush of air left my lungs at the news. I'd had a feeling that he was, but hearing it confirmed was a whole different story. I reached over to pull Ace into a hug and he lifted his hand up to stop me.

"I need to shower, but I want you to join me in the bathroom in ten minutes, completely naked."

That fluttery feeling in my stomach? Came back with a vengeance. Dangerous vibes fell off of him in droves, and I couldn't help but wonder what that would mean for whatever he had planned. He walked out of the room without another word.

I looked at my phone before lifting my wineglass to my lips again and drained the rest of my drink. I didn't move for a couple more minutes, giving him time to get into the shower and start cleaning up. With the wineglass in hand, I headed back into the kitchen and rinsed it out before setting it in the dishwasher to be washed at another time. Between Ace being okay, the promise of what was to come from him and the wine, I couldn't deny that I was feeling a buzz.

I strolled back into the bedroom and slowly undressed, partially due to my wrist and due to me wanting to waste some time before I entered the bathroom at the time he'd requested. When that task was done, I tried my best to tame my hair but soon realized that it didn't matter anyway.

A quick glance at my phone told me it had been about ten minutes. I bit my lip before I caught myself. The fluttering in my belly increased tenfold as I walked over to the bathroom door. I threw my shoulders back and stood up straight. I opened the bathroom door and stepped inside.

Ace turned to face me when I entered the room and my heart jumped into my throat. I didn't expect his stare to still have that effect on me, but it had. His presence still maintained this stronghold over me that I couldn't quite explain.

He brushed his hair back off his face before holding his hand out to me, a silent way of asking me to join him in the shower. Before taking his offer, I took off my wrist brace to avoid getting it wet and then slipped my other hand into his. When I stepped into the shower, his eyes were zeroed in on mine. He bent down to kiss me and my eyes drifted closed, enjoying the feel of his lips.

Our kiss came to an end naturally, and he took his time washing every inch of me. I would have thought he would have preferred if I helped him get cleaned up, given what had happened, but this felt like an extension of the night's events. He'd murdered someone for harming me and now he was taking care of me.

"Remember you told me that you wanted Falcone's head on a silver platter?"

I vaguely remembered it as memories of what I'd witnessed when Ian was murdered rose to the surface. "Yes."

"I should have it in a couple of hours."

My mouth dropped open, and I spluttered as some of the water got into my mouth. "You're having his head delivered here?"

"No, I'm not having it delivered here, but I made a promise to you that I wanted to keep, so if you wanted to see it, then you could."

I thought about it for a moment before I responded. "Nah, I'll take your word for it."

Ace chuckled, and I found myself smiling too. We rinsed off and he helped me out of the shower. Once we were both dried off, Ace walked me over to the bathroom counter and turned me around so that I was facing the mirror.

"Do you know what I love watching?"

Although I assumed I knew where he was going with this, I shook my head.

"Watching the way your mouth parts slightly when I do this."

He laid a kiss on my neck and I felt my mouth open slightly involuntarily.

"Just like that, sweetness. Or when I play with your nipples and you let out the low moan that I love so much."

He followed his own instructions and I couldn't prevent the groan that left my lips even if someone had paid me.

"Or when I play with this pussy and you completely lose control."

I watched as his fingers danced along my skin and landed right where I wanted them. I wondered if making love after killing the man who helped terrorize your lover was therapeutic in a way for him because it felt therapeutic for me.

He played with me, and my body involuntarily leaned into his touch as my head leaned into his chest while my back arched. When he stopped, my eyes shot open, and I glared at him through the mirror.

"Lean on your right arm," he said before placing his hand on my back and applying pressure. I felt the head of his cock teasing my entrance and I was about to beg him to fuck me when he took pity on me and entered me in one swift motion. I cried out in pleasure as my body adjusted to his cock inside me.

"Fuck," Ace mumbled behind me as his hand slapped my ass. The heat that I was getting from him pounding into me, plus the coolness from the countertop, was causing all sorts of sensations and I could feel myself reaching the point of no return.

"I'm going to—"

My words died on my lips and the only thing that I could form was a scream that seemingly bounced off the walls of the bathroom. He soon followed me with a guttural growl of his own.

We'd somehow cleaned ourselves up again and made it to bed. As I lay on his chest, enjoying the sound of his heartbeat under my ear, it lulled me into a sense of security that hadn't been there the entire time he was gone.

"I was worried about you," I said, breaking the silence that lay between us.

"It's been a long time since I've heard anyone say that."

I lifted my head and looked into his dark eyes. The hurt and pain that I saw in them now was a stark contrast to the fire that burned in his eyes when he returned from killing Falcone.

"You don't have to worry about not hearing that for as long as I walk this earth, because I'll always be concerned about your well-being. That's part of what love is."

He tightened the grip he had on me, pressing me closer to his chest. "I love you too."

I loved hearing him say it, but I had no doubt in my mind that he did.

"There's one thing I haven't been able to piece together now after tonight."

"And what's that?"

"Falcone didn't own up to ordering Emma to kidnap you."

I didn't say anything, instead choosing to stare at the

farthest corner of the room while I processed what he said. "I don't understand. Either he's lying or—"

"He's telling the truth and someone else was after you in order to get to me."

19

ACE

"The proposal looks great," I said as I looked over the documents that stood before me. I glanced up at the two people that stood before me, unable to hide their grins because of my praise. "Send this to me in an email."

"Yes, sir."

They walked away in a hurry, probably excited about this 'win'. I walked into my office and shut my office door behind me.

Finally, silence surrounded me.

I took off my suit jacket and rolled up the sleeves of my button-down as I sat down at my desk. I'd decided to come into the office today since it had been a while since I'd been there in person with Harlow's accident and recovery. It also meant that I'd had a host of in-person meetings today and it was the first time I would be sitting down at my desk for an extended period all day.

I debated calling Harlow to check in, but we had spoken via text a couple of hours earlier. While it was now a week after Falcone's death, it still made me somewhat hesitant to not be with her even though I knew she was fine. I knew she was safe because of the extra safety precautions we had in place and I mostly chalked it up to me being away from her today.

It wouldn't be too much effort for me to leave the office early and work from home. Then I wouldn't find my mind drifting as I thought about how she was or what she was doing.

My office phone ringing forced me out of my thoughts and I sighed. My quest for silence for more than two seconds had been interrupted. When I checked who was calling, I had a quick debate with myself where I weighed whether it was worth answering the phone or not but decided to do the former.

"Hello."

My grandfather didn't answer right away. In fact, I wondered if he hadn't realized he'd called me due to his lack of response to my greeting.

"Ace, how are you? How's Harlow?"

So, he had meant to reach out to me. I never would have thought that we would talk as often as we have these last few weeks. His tone was reminiscent of how he sounded when he came to the hospital when Harlow was being treated. There will never be a day when I didn't feel that my grandfather calling and sounding concerned about my well-being wasn't strange.

"We're doing great. Is there anything I can help you with?"

My grandfather cleared his throat and asked, "Remember when I asked if you would like to grab a drink with me after the board meeting?"

"Yes, I do."

"That was because I wanted to talk to you about a number of things and felt much better about doing it in person. But it wasn't the right time."

He wasn't wrong there.

"I wanted to see if you and your girlfriend would come out to my island? I'll show you around, we can talk, and you two can consider it a vacation. A way to get away from all of the drama that has happened recently. Plus, I want to get to know you and the man you've become."

Several responses came to mind as I tried to process what he'd just said. I chose one of the milder answers that I came up with. "This is strange coming from you, I must admit."

My grandfather sighed. "I admit that I've made some horrible choices in my life. I want to extend an olive branch to you and get to know you more. It's what I hoped to do when I visited New York, but with everything that had happened, I knew it wasn't the right time."

I tapped my fingertips on my desk to give me a second to think. "Let me think about it and talk to Harlow."

"That's all I want. Thank you for at least considering the offer."

"You're welcome."

"Okay, well... I'll let you go, seeing as how it's the middle of the day and you probably have plenty to do."

"Goodbye."

I hung up the phone and sat back, distracted from the tasks I should have been doing, but all I could do was replay the conversation in my mind. I couldn't remember a time when I'd heard my grandfather be unsure of himself, but after the conversation we'd just had, that was the feeling I was getting. Had the last few years mellowed him out? It was possible, but I now had a lot to think about.

"What's wrong?"

Harlow's question broke through the thoughts I was having while stirring the pasta dish she'd made with my fork. While the food was great, something else was bothering me.

"My grandfather called today and invited us to his private island."

The look on Harlow's face was comical. A range of emotions passed over her beautiful features and pretty much mirrored what I was also feeling on the inside.

"That wasn't something I was expecting you to say."

"I know. And I wanted to talk to you about it before making a decision. The fact that I'm even thinking about it this hard is a testament to my curiosity about how this will unfold and how I've softened my stance on him more recently."

Harlow took a sip of her wine and then said, "Well, if this is something you want to do, I'm in your corner one hundred and ten percent."

My lips twitched. "Is that the only reason you're in my corner?"

I watched as she bit back a grin. "I'm not going to say no to a vacation."

"Thought that might play a role in it."

Harlow reached over and grabbed my hand. "Seriously, if this is something you want to do, I'm game. I want to support you in the decisions that you need to make. If you want to go to your grandfather's private island, then we'll go. Also, I never thought I would say those words in a million years."

I chuckled and the smile on her face eased some of the tension I was feeling. Even with all the shit we'd been through, being with her was just so damn easy.

"I haven't decided if I want to go back to Beyond the Page yet and this will be the perfect opportunity to get away and think about that more."

I understood her feelings about that. After all, it was where she was almost kidnapped, which led to her getting into a car accident that could have easily been a lot worse than it was.

"He came and visited me while you were in the hospital. He also brought you flowers, but I threw them away." I'd debated whether it was worth telling her about the flowers and that it wouldn't hurt.

Harlow paused and looked up at me. "That was nice of him."

"It was, but it made me suspicious. I can't remember him going out of his way to do something that was nice for someone else in... potentially ever. I'm also concerned about how he found out you were in the hospital to begin with.'

"I'm sure word could have traveled."

She was right. Word could have traveled even though I'd thought Kingston and I had taken all the precautions we could have taken to prevent that from happening. It was easier for leaks to occur than to stop them, but my thoughts about how easy it was that this could have happened didn't remove any of the strange feelings I was having about the situation.

Harlow took her napkin from her lap and placed it on the dining room table. "Do you know why your grandfather is inviting us to his home?"

It was a question that I'd flipped over in my head multiple times myself. "I know he wants to talk with me as he tried to do after the board meeting, but I don't have any more information than that. I will say that—"

"You would say what, Ace?"

I paused for a moment before I formed a response. "He seems to be turning over a new leaf. It makes me wonder if something drastic has happened. Like he's found out something related to his health or something along those lines."

Harlow's face darkened. "You think he might be trying to make amends before he dies?"

"Wouldn't be the first time someone has done it, but speculating doesn't do us any good."

"Good point."

"I'll make the arrangements and make sure to clear as much of my work schedule as I can so that we can go."

A grin appeared on Harlow's face. She squeezed my hand and said, "Sounds like a lovely plan."

20

HARLOW

I don't think I could ever get used to riding in a private plane. The level of service and comfort was top notch and my every need was catered to. I'd always dreamed of having enough money to not have to worry about how I would pay my bills or get food on the table. This was far beyond my wildest dreams and I was grateful.

It was about a week after Ace and I had chatted about going on a tropical vacation to his grandfather's private island, and now we were on our way. I was looking forward to leaving my heavier clothes behind and instead roaming a warm oasis in the least amount of clothes while still looking presentable.

Thankfully, the flight wasn't that long, and soon our plane was taxiing to its gate. Based on the aerial view of the island, I wasn't surprised that he'd purchased the place.

From the beautiful clear waters to the sandiest of beaches, the island looked picturesque from above. If I had the money, I'd also purchase my own private island, especially if it looked like this. Given the beauty that we'd seen from above,

I could only imagine how stunning it would be once we disembarked and were out and about.

I didn't have to wait long to settle my curiosity. Ace walked out of the plane first and held my hand as I descended from the final step. I gave him a big smile while I smoothed out the wrinkles from the pink cocktail dress that I wore for the plane ride down here. Ace's outfit was simpler than mine, just a plain white button-down shirt and navy slacks, but they fit him perfectly. It had taken some strong self-restraint on my part to not beg him to take me back into the bedroom of the plane and fuck me senseless.

No, I needed to be as presentable as possible for when I met Ace's grandfather and I wasn't sure when that would take place. Although I didn't think that Ace held his grandfather's opinion in high regard, I couldn't stop myself from wanting to make a good impression. Not to mention, I was thankful for the flowers he'd given me when I was recovering from the car accident in the hospital. It was a nice gesture even if I hadn't gotten a chance to see them and Ace was wondering about whether ulterior motives were at play.

We were greeted by Ace's grandfather's driver, and soon, we were headed to meet him.

I grabbed Ace's hand and gave it a small squeeze. "Do you know what your grandfather's house looks like?"

Ace shook his head. "You and I are both experiencing this for the first time. I've never been here."

That made sense, given the rift between Ace and his grandfather. I hoped this was a way for them to potentially come to terms with their estrangement and compromise so that they could build a relationship with one another. As someone who grew up in foster care and didn't feel like I belonged anywhere, it was overly important to me to foster relationships with non-toxic family members while they were here. If Ace had more doubts about his grandfather or didn't want to come, I would have respected his answer. But because he was interested in coming here, I respected that as well. After all, this might now be the start of a beautiful relationship between the two.

After settling the thoughts I had about the situation in my mind, at least for now, I turned to Ace. "Are you going to bring up anything with him, or will you just let him do all of the talking?"

Ace looked up and stared at the driver instead of responding right away. Shit. It made sense that he didn't want the driver, who was more than likely loyal to his grandfather, to overhear any specific details of our conversation.

"I do have some matters that I want to discuss with him."

I nodded and gave him a reassuring smile. If Ace was going to be doing some of the talking, then this would probably also be a good experience for him.

Ace and I weren't much different in certain aspects of our lives. Yes, he had more money than I could've ever dreamed of, but we were both thrown to the wolves in different aspects of our lives and fought to see the other side. If this whole meeting went to shit, I hoped it would bring him some closure with part of his childhood and lead to answers about why he ended up where he had. It's something I wish I could do, but I was happy to be here, helping him find it.

He grabbed my hand and held it in his but did nothing more. It was as if it was a comfort thing for him, and I was happy to oblige.

The ride to our vacation home wasn't long and when our

driver pointed out where we would be staying, my mouth dropped open. The home was stunning. If this was one of Jerald's residences and not his main home on the island, I could only imagine how big his permanent residence was.

The tan home was stunning and had a lot of flowers and greenery outside of it. Between the colorful flowers and the smell of the ocean breeze, everything about this place screamed island paradise and I could feel my body relaxing with every breath I took.

"You know if I was retiring here, I would have left New York City quick, fast, and in a hurry too."

I didn't realize I said the sentence out loud until I heard Ace laughing beside me.

"I can see what you mean."

This time I looked over at him and asked, "Does it make you want to buy your own private island?"

"Is that what you want?"

His question caused heat to rise in my cheeks. "I wouldn't mind a tropical getaway."

"Duly noted."

Ace reached over and lifted my chin with his finger. My eyes fluttered closed as we both leaned in to seal our conversation with a kiss.

"Ace, I can't get over any of this. This place is immaculate."

We'd pulled up to where we would be staying about twenty minutes ago and were given a quick tour of the house. Everything about this place was beautiful and I knew I was going to enjoy my stay. I'd already had my eye on the outdoor pool and knew I was going to spend a lot of time out there between lounging in the pool and swimming up to the bar.

"Get changed, and we can go to the beach or the pool."

There was nothing that could stop a smile from appearing on my face. "Are you sure?"

Ace nodded. "When we walked past the pool, you looked as if you might say to hell with it all and dive in, so yes. It might be easier to get some light refreshments there to hold us over until dinner."

"Are we having dinner with your grandfather this evening?" I wanted to make sure I had the correct information because if I was being honest, I'd been half paying attention to what was being told to me while we were touring the property.

"That's correct."

"Okay, the pool it is. I'm going to change and then we can head down."

Ace gave me a small, lazy smile as he walked over to me. "We're going to change and then we'll head down together."

I lifted my head so that he could kiss my lips. When we broke apart, I said, "I didn't expect you to want to go swimming."

"Why is that?"

"Because you didn't do it at your house upstate? I got more usage out of your pool when I was there than you did."

"That's not true."

I did a double take. "Wait, what?"

Ace took a small step back and began to unbutton his white shirt. "While I didn't swim daily, I did early in the morning while you were still asleep. Now, Harlow, you might want to close your mouth and change into your bathing suit. You're catching flies."

All I could do was stare at him with my mouth slightly open. I guessed you really did learn something new every day.

21

ACE

As the sun began to set, I couldn't get enough of the beautiful scenery that we passed on the way to my grandfather's home. After an afternoon spent in the sun, it was time for dinner, and I wouldn't lie and say that this was something I was looking forward to.

While my grandfather and I had never gotten into fights from what I could remember, that didn't mean that things wouldn't get intense due to the tension that we had been harboring between us for as long as I could remember. Plus, we were on his turf now, so who knew how much that changed the stakes.

Harlow placed her hand on my thigh and gave me a warm smile. Although the gesture was innocent in nature, it did cause me to think of that hand wrapped around my cock as I fucked her mouth.

Calm down, Ace. You don't want to go into your grandfather's home as hard as a damn rock.

The images, however, did take my mind off what felt like

Harlow and me walking into the devil's den. And nothing I did could help me shake that feeling.

There was no indication that this was anything other than an innocent dinner, but I still couldn't shake the feeling that something was amiss about it.

As we were pulling up to my grandfather's home, I pulled out my phone and looked at the screen. I'd called a few people while I was waiting for Harlow to finish getting ready and I was curious to see if anyone had tried to reach out to me, but no one had. I put my phone away and turned to Harlow just before our driver for the evening put the car in park. The sun was casting a beautiful glow around her, highlighting her hair and the smile that played on her lips. I tucked a piece of her hair behind her ear and she leaned into my touch.

Our moment was interrupted when the car pulled up to what had to be the largest house on the island. My grandfather had truly outdone himself, but that was also not surprising, given our lineage.

The outside of this house was like the home we were staying in but on steroids. It had to be almost double, if not triple, the size, and that was just based on what we were seeing from the outside. I didn't know how far back it went or the other amenities on the property, but based on first impressions, it was clear that my grandfather had spent his time building what could be deemed the perfect sanctuary on this island.

Our driver opened my door first before heading over to Harlow and helping her out of the car as I walked around the back of the vehicle. This time, while it was clear that Harlow was in shock, she did a better job of masking it by keeping her mouth shut.

We thanked our driver before she tucked her arm around mine and we began to walk up the stairs to the house.

"You know," Harlow started to whisper to me. "I thought you lived a very extravagant lifestyle, but this is something else entirely."

That was the understatement of the year. The excitement from looking at such a beautiful home took away from the thoughts I was having in the car on the way here until I watched the door of said home slowly open.

I'd expected my grandfather to have a butler that would open the door, but when I saw that it was him in the doorway, I was slightly taken aback, although I refused to show it. Not showing much emotion seemed to be a Bolton family trait that we'd perfected which was another reason why my grandfather showing any other form of emotion, including concern, was strange.

"Welcome, welcome!" my grandfather said with open arms. "Please come in."

Harlow slightly clung to my arm, showing me that we both hadn't expected this warm of a greeting from the man standing in front of us.

We walked through the front door and I was shocked by what greeted me on the inside. This place was nothing like the estate back in New York. Where the home that I bought from him was dark and gloomy, this place had so much vibrancy that I wondered if the decor choices had been approved by the same person. It seemed as if he took a lot of inspiration from his surroundings because it was obvious to see that the environment on the outside had served as a muse for the color palette used on the inside. It fit the home perfectly. Even the warm breeze blowing in through the open windows was perfect.

"I swear everything on this island is stunning, Mr. Bolton."

Harlow's soft voice broke through my thoughts and I turned my head to look at her. Her grip on my arm had lessened, showing me that she wasn't as stressed about being here as she was when we were walking up the steps.

"Thank you so much, dear. And please call me Jerald."

I dragged my attention back to my grandfather and stared him down. While I didn't trust too many people, I was willing to give them the benefit of the doubt when it came to a shift in behavior. But having my grandfather act in a manner that was the exact opposite of what I was used to from him was fucking with me. My instincts told me I needed to stay on guard because something wasn't right about the situation.

My grandfather held out his hand for him to shake Harlow's and when he held onto hers for a little too long, I cleared my throat. He backed away with a small smile on his face, telling me that he knew exactly what he was doing. What the hell was he doing?

"Dinner should be served momentarily. Can I get you both a drink and we can take them out on the balcony and watch the sun continue to set?"

Harlow nodded eagerly while giving my grandfather a large grin. My reaction was more tepid, and I decided to take more of a wait-and-see approach before I got excited about anything.

When my grandfather turned and walked away to go and

grab the drinks, Harlow grinned at me. "I don't know what I had been expecting, but it wasn't this."

I had to agree with her on that. None of this was out of his normal playbook. I was also willing to bet that Harlow's reaction to this was related to the experiences she had as a result of being put up for adoption and then losing Mama Robinson once she had found a loving home. She longed for the family she didn't have when she was put into foster care and she longed for the family she lost when Mama Robinson died. But what she didn't realize was that whatever was going on here stunk to high heaven, and I was determined to find out why.

Part of me wanted to hightail it out of here right now with Harlow, but I knew that meant I wouldn't get the answers that I wanted. Playing it cool right now was my best option and setting up contingency plans just in case something happened was a must. It never hurt to be overprepared, and I needed to be in order to stay several steps in front of my grandfather.

I leaned down and pretended like I was nibbling on Harlow's neck, but instead I whispered in her ear, "Stay alert while you're here, and be careful of anything you eat or drink here. I don't think there's anything wrong with it, but you can never be too sure."

She looked at me quizzically but didn't have a chance to say anything because we both turned to find my grandfather approaching us. One drink was in his hand and someone else who must have worked on the property had the other drinks in his hands.

Once we'd been given our drinks and the three of us were

alone again, my grandfather raised his glass. "To a wonderful time in paradise."

"Cheers," Harlow said before the three of us clinked glasses with one another. I noticed that her enthusiasm for being here had waned, but I didn't think my grandfather had realized. I put the drink to my lips and pretended to take a sip. I glanced over my shoulder and saw that Harlow's eyes were on me and that she had done the same.

Good girl.

Our dinners were served and while I assumed both Harlow and I were hungry, we didn't make a big show of it. We politely took a few bites of the food in front of us, but the lingering thoughts of whether the food had been poisoned still remained.

My grandfather did most of the talking and although he tried to hide his annoyance about us not eating dinner, he didn't outright ask why we were essentially shoving food around the plate. We'd have to take a risk in eating the food in our vacation home, but I thought taking away any thunder from an event where we could get sick in his primary residence was key.

I cleared my throat and sat back in the dining room chair, pretending I'd finished eating as a result of my still very full plate. "That was delicious, but I'm stuffed. Did you want to start a discussion about why you wanted us to come here?"

My grandfather waved me off. "Oh, it can wait. I wanted to just welcome you here to start your vacation off with a lovely dinner."

My irritation started to grow because this seemed like it was a big game to him. My grandfather was normally a person who had no problem getting to the point because he didn't like wasting time, especially his own. I knew this was a stalling technique to show that he was the one running the show here, not me. Too bad I had news for him.

"Well, if this is it, Harlow and I should head back to rest for the evening. We spent quite a bit of time traveling and I assume we are both tired."

Harlow nodded and gave a pleasant smile that showed none of the natural warmth she carried around with her. She wanted to get out of here as much as I did.

"Very well. Let me walk you to the door then."

My grandfather did as he said he would and nothing suspicious happened between us leaving his dining room table and exiting the front door.

"It was lovely having dinner with you, Jerald."

My grandfather turned to Harlow and gave her a smile. "It was a complete pleasure. I'll see you both soon."

Once we were settled in the car and our driver pulled away from the curb, my grandfather stood out near his driveway and watched us as our car pulled off, like a concerned grandparent making sure to see us off. But I knew that was a lie.

22

HARLOW

My hands tightened the belt of my robe as I stood on the balcony looking out onto the morning sunrise, I couldn't help but close my eyes as the light breeze swept over my body. I'd left a sleeping Ace in the bedroom to take the opportunity to enjoy a quiet sunrise by myself. This had to be one of the most peaceful places on the planet. Although not being in New York felt weird, I wondered if I could get used to this.

Drifting between relaxing on the beach and lounging by the pool were the hardest choices I would have to make over the next few days and I wasn't complaining. We'd made plans to visit other places on the island later today and I couldn't wait to see the sights. The only thing that had made me a little nervous was the possibility that Jerald would show up as our guide.

So far, dinner at Ace's grandfather's house had been the only downside to this trip. To be fair, it was only a minor inconvenience, thankfully.

Things were awkward as we drove to Jerald's house. I

didn't expect anything less because I was meeting Ace's only living family member for the first time. Then my nerves were shot to hell after Ace told me to be wary around his grandfather.

With Ace's warning in the back of my mind, I had to say that dinner was a success and nothing out of the ordinary happened. Did I think that Ace was overreacting? No, because I trusted him enough to believe that something had triggered him to have this response. Now what had been the catalyst, I wasn't sure, and we hadn't had a chance to speak about it after getting home from dinner last night. I also suspected that Ace wanted to keep conversations about his grandfather to a minimum while we stayed on his property anyway and I didn't blame him. Who knew who might over-hear what we were talking about? So that made things some-what difficult as well.

"Harlow."

I looked over my shoulder and found Ace standing there. His eyes narrowed and his hair stuck up in all different directions.

"What are you doing out here?"

"Looking for you," Ace said as he walked out onto the balcony. He wrapped his hands around my waist and pulled me into his chest. "Why are you standing out here?"

"I thought watching the sunrise might be fun and a way to catch my breath with everything going on."

"Are you referring to dinner last night?" The volume of his voice dropped, yet it wasn't quite a whisper.

I nodded my head in case he didn't want me to respond out loud. There were so many more questions I wanted to ask, but before I could, Ace stopped me.

The light kisses on my neck as we watched the morning sky were all I wanted and needed. There would be a time later on when I could have all of my questions answered.

The kisses turned into something deeper and I squealed when Ace took a small step back before spinning me around and closing in on me again. The light reflected off of his dark eyes just before his eyes lowered to study my lips. When he leaned down to kiss me, every fiber of my being felt as if it was on fire and he'd only kissed me.

When our kiss ended and he stepped back again, I didn't know what to expect. The smirk on his lips should have been a hint because before I could blink, Ace had thrown me over his shoulder and walked back inside of the bedroom.

My giggles filled the air as I lay upside down on his shoulder, and it was until he tossed me onto the bed that I noticed the wicked look in his eyes. With one swift motion, he tore open my robe, exposing my naked body to his hungry gaze. He ripped the belt of the robe off my body and looked at me.

"Do you remember your safe word?"

I sat up on my elbows and nodded so quickly I looked like a bobblehead doll. "Lavender."

"Good girl."

I nearly came right there.

As he moved toward me again, I held out my hand to stop him. "Aren't you worried someone might hear or see us? Given the fact that we've been... trying to be more discrete with our conversations?"

"I'm pretty sure there are no cameras in here, but I was worried about listening devices. And to that, I say let's give them a show, because there's no way I'm not fucking you right now. Open your legs."

I could feel my heart begin to race. I opened my legs wider as Ace approached me with the belt. He tied the belt around my head, covering my eyes so that I couldn't see. Here I lay, as naked as the day I was born, wondering what he would do next. It reminded me of when I'd joined the mile-high club with him on our trip to Utah.

I strained my ears to hear any sounds that might indicate what he was up to but the only thing I heard was some muffled footsteps as he moved around the room.

When the bed dipped under his weight to the right of me, I licked my lips in anticipation of what was to come.

I felt his tongue take my nipple into his mouth and I arched my back to force my breast toward him. His fingers found my core and began teasing me there. It seemed as if he had no intention of wasting any time when it came to getting down to business.

"You don't know how exquisite you look right now. Your nipples are as hard as pebbles, your pussy glistening in the early light of the sunrise."

His words and motions forced a shiver out of me and when he slid one of his fingers into me, I moaned. I tried to grind my hips into his hand and didn't care that it made me look desperate for his touch.

"Do you need two fingers, sweetness?"

"Fuck, yes." My words came out slurred, almost as if I was drunk. Hell, maybe I was. Drunk on him.

"Your wish has been granted." When he slid his second finger in, he growled. "Your pussy is so tight, baby."

Right now, he could tell me that the sky was green and I would believe him.

He sucked on my nipple one last time before letting it go

with a resounding 'pop' before he said, "Lie down on your back."

I moved my elbows to follow his directions and I could feel him lift my legs. The next thing I felt was his tongue on my pussy. I moved my hands toward where I knew he was and clumsily fingered his hair, encouraging him to keep going because if he stopped, I would be highly upset.

The rhythm of his tongue and fingers was enough to send me spiraling out of control and I found myself trying to ride his fingers to get me to my climax faster. Soon it felt as if I'd won the ultimate prize as my body careened out of control as my orgasm flowed through me.

"That's one."

"Wait, what—"

My words were cut off when Ace removed his mouth and fingers from me. I felt what I assumed was the head of his cock, teasing my slit up and down, coating himself in my juices. When he slipped his dick into me, he growled as we both enjoyed the connection that we now had to one another. He gave me a second to adjust before he pulled his cock almost all the way out before pounding into me.

"Oh my—" All I knew was that my brain felt as if it were short-circuiting and this felt like I was coasting on cloud nine.

When he did it again, my cry turned into a groan as my hands made their way to the sheets on the bed because that was the only thing I could grab on to. His body found a rhythm that was much faster, and I knew it was only a matter of time before I exploded again.

The sounds that were coming out of my mouth were incoherent and that seemed to only further encourage Ace to keep going. When I came all over his cock again, I fought to catch my breath as Ace slowed down. What I didn't know was that it would be temporary.

"That was number two."

"I don't think I can come any more." My words came out between harsh breathing.

"Is that a challenge?"

"That isn't what I meant—" I truly didn't think I could again, but that was when I realized he still hadn't come.

"So, it is a challenge. I choose to accept."

I felt Ace lean over me and then he said, "I've always wanted to make love to you with the sound of waves in the background and the time for that will come. But we're going to do something a little different."

Ace removed the belt from my head and it took me a second to adjust to the light in the room again. He took that opportunity to roll his hips before he surged into me again. A moan fell from my lips. Staring into his dark eyes added another dimension to our lovemaking.

What I hadn't been expecting was for him to grab a vibrator. Where he'd hidden it would remain a mystery for now. When he placed it on my pussy, I cried out in surprise even though I had seen it coming.

Having him fuck me while using the vibrator on me caused so many sensations that I couldn't even begin to describe. I looked at Ace and saw the intensity in his eyes, the desire to bring out another orgasm from me was evident. My head shot back, and I screamed again as I clenched the sheets between my fingers for moral support. He was obviously determined to give me another orgasm by any means necessary, and I loved him for it.

Once again, it felt as if all of the nerves in my body were ablaze as he slammed into me while using the toy.

"Give it to me, Harlow," he grunted between thrusts.

I could feel my walls contracting around his cock and I knew this time I was going to be the one granting his wish. I gasped for air as I felt my body trembling from his assault on it. This orgasm coursed through me, much harder than the last two and I knew I was spent. He turned off the vibrator and tossed it onto the bed before grabbing my hips.

He thrust once and then twice before he roared, announcing that he too had gone past the point of no return.

I tried to look up at him, but my eyes refused to open. I was so tired from our activities that there was no way I was opening my eyes, let alone attempting to move anywhere.

Ace must have known because he helped move my limp body up toward the head of the bed and somehow managed to get us both under the covers. I used the last bit of my energy to open my eyes slightly and throw myself onto his chest.

"Well, that was a way to get the morning started."

Ace let out a belly laugh that caused me to giggle against his chest.

"I'd have to agree with that, Harlow. I'd have to agree."

23

ACE

It was our last evening at my grandfather's private island. After a week of fun in the sun and time spent with one another, it was time to leave paradise and return to the real world.

When my grandfather invited us back to his home for a late lunch, it wasn't a surprise to me. After all, we never accomplished the real reason he wanted me to come here, and that was to discuss something only he knew.

In order to get the most out of our day, Harlow and I decided to do a small round of shopping so that she could pick up a couple of things, including some small souvenirs for Marnie, Anderson, and Chanel. The plan was for us to go shopping, then head back to the vacation home to drop things off and then head to my grandfather's.

Before we could step into the car that would take us to our home away from home, I received a text message from Kingston.

Kingston: *The side project you wanted me to work on? I found all of the details you wanted. Sending you an email with every-thing as an attachment.*

Harlow was busy buckling her seat belt, so she didn't notice the grin on my face. I couldn't wait to blow her mind with this latest surprise.

I masked my emotions and put on my own seat belt as the car pulled away from the curb of the vacation home. Harlow and I made small talk during the entire drive that didn't veer into talking about my grandfather. We'd found time to talk somewhere more private, where I explained everything that I thought about this situation with him and why it was troubling. She agreed with me and I was glad that we were both on the same page regarding this.

I scrolled through my messages to see if Parker had answered the last message I sent him, but there was nothing. That was an irritation that I didn't want to deal with right now.

The drive had been quick and uneventful. When the driver parked in front of the vacation home, I told him we would only be a few minutes before he got out of the car to open the door for Harlow and me. I took the bags from Harlow before placing my hand on the small of her back to guide her into the house.

We'd grown to expect that one of the staffers that my grandfather had hired to keep up the residence would open the door, but instead it was a huge guy dressed all in black. Every fiber of my being was on high alert as I tried my best to prevent Harlow and me from entering the building while also trying to shield her from any harm that came her way. I was successful in one area and not the other because the driver of the vehicle we just rode in had come up the rear and was blocking any attempt we had of trying to escape that way. I managed to brush against my phone twice before the guy who had been our driver on the island drew his gun, forcing both Harlow and me to put our hands up.

Our former driver gestured for us to enter the home and we did as requested. It came as no surprise that I found my grandfather standing over the threshold. The door shut behind us, effectively closing us off from the outside world.

"What the hell is all of this about?" It was easy to tell I was pissed, partially because we came here and also because I'd suspected that something like this might happen after we arrived. But when nothing had happened, I let my guard slip and now here we were. I should have tried to get us out of there ASAP, but I hadn't. Now, we had to suffer the consequences.

"We needed to have a chat, and I thought this was the perfect opportunity to have one," my grandfather said.

"But we were on our way to your house anyway. You could have cornered us there."

"That would have been easier, yes. But coming here, when you least expected it, made this all the more interesting, hasn't it?"

"Your idea of what makes something interesting is completely fucked up."

My grandfather didn't have an answer for that. Instead, he held out his hand to one of the other men in the foyer and was handed a gun.

"What do you want? You wouldn't do this without having a reason, so tell me."

"I want to kill her."

Harlow gasped behind me, but I showed no reaction. I

was still blocking her with my body, trying to map out a plan to get us out of here alive and uninjured. "Why do you want to kill her?"

"Because she'll only serve as a distraction to you as you continue to grow in your role as president and CEO."

That hadn't been what I expected him to say, so to say I was shocked was putting it mildly. "Are you fucking kidding me?"

He looked serious. Dead serious. "Your mother was supposed to take over for me once I retired. I knew she would eventually have children, so then the family business would be passed on, keeping our family's legacy alive. But then she got pregnant with you way earlier than she should have. I knew that you would become her entire world and that she wouldn't give a damn about anything related to the family business."

That's when some things started to click in my head. "So that's why you kicked her out of the house."

He nodded, confirming my assumption. How he could do such a thing for that reason was mind boggling.

"That was part of the reason. The other reason was because I was pretty sure she'd gotten pregnant as a result of fucking one of my business rivals at the time."

I held back the anger that was simmering just below the surface. It was the only way I was going to get the answers that I deserved. Thankfully it seemed as if he had no problem talking about all of our family's history, and it was hopefully buying some more time for my contingency plan to get into place. If it had worked. "How do you know that?"

"Because it lined up with a party that Kiki was throwing

at The Sphynx that I knew your mother had attended because I saw her there."

When the information I was receiving started clicking together, it almost took on a snowball effect as everything started to come together. My grandfather's connection to Falcone, us trying to hunt down Falcone at The Sphynx. "You were the one that called a meeting with Falcone at The Sphynx, weren't you?"

My grandfather gave me the biggest smile he'd ever given me in my entire life. "You're right on the money there, son. It also sent you on a wild-goose chase. I heard about how you didn't catch him then, but I applaud you for killing him at Bar 53. Nice touch killing him on his own property."

I thought about how I would absolutely not have the same issue doing it here, but the goal was to keep him talking, all the while guarding Harlow with my body. I wanted to look behind me to see if she was okay, but I refused to take my eyes off any of the men in this room.

"And you organized Harlow's kidnapping. It was also how you knew that she was in the hospital."

He nodded his head slowly as if he was judging my response. "Emma was recommended to me by Falcone after you bought Harlow at the auction. He told me she would easily do something like what I wanted for a little cash. The icing on the cake was when she stole money from Falcone before helping your girl find a place to live.

"So why didn't you just kill her then? You knew where she was hiding and it would have been easy."

His grin turned dark. "Because I was hoping that Ian would get to her first. Consider it a punishment of sorts, but you stopped that from occurring."

And that was when the stone-cold truth was staring me dead in the face. If he knew that Ian would try to rape Harlow if given the chance, then...

"You knew what Kiki would do to me when you said you didn't want me to live with you, didn't you?"

This time my grandfather shrugged. "I had my suspicions. It was easy to piece two and two together."

"All those years you could have done something to save me, and you left me with her, knowing damn well what she was doing. You're a sick fuck."

"It was to teach you both a lesson."

"A lesson about what!" I couldn't contain my emotions any longer.

"It was to teach you how to become a man. To show you that the most important thing in this world was to keep our business afloat because, without It, we are nothing. It should have taught you not to settle ever, in your professional life or in your personal life. Plus, Kiki having to be your guardian was her punishment for introducing your mother to things she shouldn't have been involved in."

"You're so full of shit."

This time my grandfather sneered at me. "I'm the one that's full of shit? You're the one that went off and fell in love with Harlow, someone who shouldn't have been more than the pussy of the day."

I glanced at Harlow as her lip trembled at his words. "Don't ever say her fucking name again."

"And you just proved my point. Now that we've had our little discussion, it's time for her to die, and I'll take great pleasure in being the one to pull the trigger. Step aside, son."

"Absolutely not. If you're going to try to kill her, then you're going to have to go through me."

"Are you letting her get between us? I gave you everything!"

I could hear the roar in my ears before it came out of my mouth. "You gave me nothing! Everything that you supposedly gave me had to do with you and keeping your legacy alive. You didn't give a fuck about me. Never have and never will, and the same goes both ways."

I felt betrayed in a way I hadn't been expecting. I knew that my grandfather cared about nothing but himself, but there was a small bit of hope where I had thought there was a possibility that I might have been wrong, especially with his change in behavior. The potential to have the family that I'd lost when he invited me to his island to go on vacation and to spend some time with him. Deep down, I knew it was a lie. A fantasy I'd made up in my head, but I hadn't fully believed it until now.

"Move the fuck out of the way, Ace. I have no problem shooting you first and then killing her. That way, you can also watch her die."

"Looks like that is just what you're going to have to do."

As my grandfather aimed the gun toward me, a shot rang out and it took a second before I realized that it hadn't come from my grandfather's gun. Harlow screamed as one of my grandfather's men fell over in a pool of their own blood, and before I could come to terms with it, there was another shot that rang out, and I saw that our former driver had been shot in the head and had fallen into the wall. Not only had it shocked me, but it had shocked my grandfather too. However,

I recovered first and was able to tackle him at full speed, causing the gun to fly out of his hand. My plan had worked.

My grandfather never had a chance to recover as I threw punch after punch at him, causing his face to become a bloody mess. My focus was on making him hurt as much as he'd made me and Harlow hurt, and it wasn't until I heard Harlow shouting at me that my attention went to her. She walked over to me as I stood up and handed me my grandfather's gun. I pointed it at the bloody mess that was on the floor.

"You know," my grandfather said as he struggled to breathe. "I always knew you were more like your mother."

"I'll take that as a compliment." And deep down, I knew she would have no problem with what I was about to do right now.

Without a second thought, I pulled the trigger, ending the misery that he had bestowed on me and others.

I pulled Harlow toward me, shielding her as her body shook in my embrace. I never imagined that I would be the one to kill my grandfather, but I would do it any day of the week to keep Harlow safe.

Suddenly, the front door opened, and I quickly moved Harlow behind me and aimed the gun at the door in case someone else was coming to harm us. I only lowered the gun when I saw who it was.

"You know how to make an entrance."

Parker Townsend walked into my grandfather's house and took in the scene before him. "Not too bad for someone who doesn't do this all that often anymore. Are you both okay?"

I pulled Harlow close and tucked her into my arms once

more. "I think so, just a little startled, that's all. Glad you were able to get here undetected."

"All in a day's work."

He didn't elaborate on how he'd managed that feat and when I looked down at Harlow, any thoughts of questioning Parker had vanished. She was in my arms, shaking like a leaf. I'd once again dragged her into a situation that she shouldn't have been involved in. It was because of me that she was here. "This is all my fault."

Harlow took a deep breath and looked up at me before she said, "Stop blaming yourself for this, Ace. You didn't know and acted in the best way you could have with the information you had at the time. No one is perfect."

Her words were soothing but still didn't remove the pain I had for dragging her into this. Then again, if we hadn't come here, wouldn't the cycle have just continued until my grandfather got what he wanted? More than likely.

Parker took a step toward us, and we both looked at him. "I talked to Kingston hours ago and Cross Sentinel should be here within the hour to clean up."

I looked down at Harlow and based on the look in her eyes, I could tell she felt the same way as me. Those were just the words that we wanted to hear.

24

HARLOW

Silence wasn't a welcome reprieve because it allowed my thoughts to run wild in my head. But neither I nor Ace spoke to each other as we drove to our next location.

This was all about closing one door so that we could open another one and deep down, I couldn't wait to, no matter how much this would initially hurt.

I skimmed the obituary that had been put together to honor Ace's grandfather as we rode to the address on the GPS. It mentioned that he'd died of natural causes and was cremated per his wishes, none of which was true. I did have to admit that the piece was wonderfully put together and even mentioned that he was survived by his loving grandson. Ace and I knew that that was a lie, but the rest of the world didn't need to know. Owning a private island where you keep things quiet, much liked he'd hoped to do with my death had its perks.

We pulled up to a warehouse in what seemed like the middle of nowhere and Ace put the car in park. Both of us sat there looking straight ahead at the structure in front of us before Ace turned to look at me and broke the silence barrier that had been in place since we left our home.

"Are you sure you want to do this?"

"Definitely. After all the things your grandfather said, I need to do this for closure. She doesn't even know I survived the car accident, does she?"

"As far as I know, she doesn't. Are you ready for this?"

I dipped my head and looked at my fingers. "As ready as I'll ever be. I want to get in and get out as quickly as possible."

Ace patted my knee before undoing his seat belt and exiting the car. I waited a beat before I undid mine as well. He opened my door and held out his hand to help me out of the car. I guessed it was pretty obvious that I was a mess and that things looked quite shaky for me at the moment.

While I had no physical ailments from our time on what was now Ace's private island, facing what lay before me in this warehouse had shaken me to my core. The mental preparation that I'd gone through to prepare me for this moment didn't seem nearly as effective as I thought it would be, but it was better to get this over with than to waste another moment thinking about it over and over again.

Once my feet were firmly on the ground, I squared my shoulders and walked into the warehouse with my head held high. There was no way anyone in here would see me slouching.

The warehouse was nothing to write home about. It was pretty barren in the same vein that it was when I was here when Ian was brought here. It felt somewhat strange to me that there were no signs of Ian's murder taking place here, but that meant that Cross Sentinel was excellent at cleaning up after a job. I shook my head at myself because I was starting to sound like Ace.

Kingston walked over to us and shook my hand and then Ace's. "We can bring Emma in now."

"Yes. Please," I said.

When Kingston walked away to go get her, I felt Ace's touch on my lower back, reminding me that he was there for me, every step of the way.

When they dragged Emma in, in handcuffs, she had her head down, looking at the ground. When she finally looked up and saw me, I watched as a startled expression appeared on her face as if she'd just seen a ghost. It only lasted a couple of seconds before she looked down at her shoes again. She'd truly thought that I had died in that car accident and no one had told her I hadn't.

When she didn't make any move to speak, I decided that silence would be a waste of time, so I spoke up. "I can't believe you did all this shit, Emma. It would have been so easy for you to tell Ace or me what you knew. Instead, money was so much more powerful to you than our friendship."

She gave no inclination that she heard me, but I knew she had.

Since she didn't bother to say anything, I continued. "I could have died, and you didn't give a fuck. After all we'd been through working at Bar 53, you had no problem throwing that all away for a quick buck. Who does that?"

Once again, she didn't respond, instead choosing to continue to focus on the ground. But her reactions to this didn't matter. Getting this off my chest felt therapeutic. I was angry as hell, but it felt good to toss all of this out there because I'd made a vow to myself that once I walked out of this room, I wouldn't give her a second thought. Because she was in my past and I was determined to walk into my future with my head held high.

"You don't realize how much this hurts me. How much you hurt me by being a lying, thieving, backstabbing bitch. And even though I know you are all of those things; this still hurts like hell."

Emma didn't say anything in response, instead choosing to continue her staring contest with the ground. Given what Ace told me about how she'd responded to him, it was interesting to see her take this approach with me.

"Do you want us to kill her?" Kingston asked.

It felt strange, once again having the power over whether someone lived or died. Her head shot up and I could see the fear in her eyes.

"I'm... sorry."

It was the first time she'd spoken since I'd gotten there and her apology meant nothing to me. Because it was then that I realized that she no longer meant anything to me.

Instead of responding to her, I looked at Kingston. "No, I don't want you to kill her. Whether she stays a prisoner of Cross Sentinel for the rest of her life is up to you guys, but I think she should live with all that she did daily. I want her to think about the fucked-up shit she did every second of every day and realize how much of a shitty person she is."

"Harlow, please. Maybe there's something I can do..."

The plea in Emma's voice sounded sincere and would be enough to pull at my heart strings if I didn't know that she was a liar and an asshole. Something inside me snapped.

"You've done enough, trust me. You know throughout my time at the auction, staying with Ace the first time and after you'd helped me hide in Dalhurst all I could think about was you. Wondering how you were, if you were okay and if there was anything I could do to help you. And you were doing this shit behind my back."

She didn't have a response for that so I continued.

"I couldn't care less about what happens to you now. So, if they want to keep you in a cell for you to rot for the rest of your life, so be it. While I didn't ask them to kill you in front of me today, you are still fucking dead to me."

I turned my back on Emma to give my full and undivided attention to Ace. "Take me home."

EPILOGUE
HARLOW

I looked at my hair in the mirror as I placed it into a high ponytail. I debated whether it was worth cutting off an inch or two and maybe cutting my hair into bangs to switch things up a bit. After all, having a new hairstyle would fit into the new life I was trying to lead. Leaving the bullshit behind me while embracing the new me and the ones that I cared about. And all of that would start once I got a look at the renovations that had been done to the properties on Ace's new private tropical paradise.

It was fitting that Ace's grandfather left him his island. It was clear that he was all about keeping shit in the family when it benefited him and not anyone else. Too bad this benefited both of us and we were planning on taking a vacation there in a couple of days.

I'd been busy handling a lot of the renovations for both our homes in upstate New York and on the island. It was definitely keeping me busy until I returned to work at Beyond the Page. What my schedule would look like when I returned to work there, we didn't know yet, but I knew that we would figure it out together.

In the end, it all worked out. Even with the traumatic events that had occurred on that island, I still fell in love with it and Ace was more than happy to keep the island because it made me happy.

I heard the front door close, and I held my breath as I waited for the person who made my heart skip a beat to speak.

"Are you ready to go, sweetness? We have reservations in about fifteen minutes."

Just hearing his voice excited me. I smiled at myself in the mirror before I responded, "I'll be there in a minute!"

Ace had talked me into going out to lunch with him a couple of blocks away from our place in the city. It was where we'd been staying more and more, especially with the renovations that were occurring. He'd even bought out the rest of our floor so that Marnie and Anderson had their own space here while the construction was going on. He even mentioned taking them to his private island with their families, if they wished to go, for some rest and relaxation as part of a thank you for being so supportive over the years. In my mind, it was a fantastic gesture along with the monetary ones he also gave them.

I smoothed down the red cocktail dress I was wearing and added lipstick to my lips. The dress reminded me a bit of the dress I'd worn when I first met Ace at the auction.

It felt good to dress up for the first time in a while because I hadn't had the opportunity to do so. Plus, I wanted it to be a small surprise for Ace because he'd gone away on a business trip and had just gotten back a couple of hours ago. Maybe my outfit might be enough to entice him that his time was better spent making up to me for lost time, instead of doing some work he swore he had to do when he called me as he was being driven back home.

After one final glance in the mirror, I walked into the living area and found Ace standing there. I drank him in as much as he was staring at me. The grin on his face was contagious because I couldn't help but smile back at him.

"Hi, handsome," I said as I walked up to him.

He pulled me into his arms and it felt like I was home even though I wasn't the one who spent part of this week out of the state.

He leaned down and gave me a kiss that he quickly deepened. Maybe it wouldn't take much convincing to get him to play hooky from work. When he moved his back, stopping our kiss, I almost whined.

"Wait, I got some lipstick on you. Probably wasn't the best choice for me to throw this on when I knew that you would probably kiss me senseless."

Ace shook his head before stopping so that I could get the makeup off of him. When I was done, he said, "I have something to share with you."

"Oh. What is it?"

"Open the front door and you'll find out."

I raised an eyebrow at Ace as I walked to the front door. *What the hell was he up to?*

"Is this a surprise or a prank?"

He gave me a pointed look. "When have I ever—"

"I know. I know." I rolled my eyes, but it did nothing to lessen the pull in my gut. *What the hell was going on?*

There was only one way to find out.

I walked away from Ace and over to the front door. I found a woman who I didn't recognize standing at the door.

I tentatively smiled at her and asked, "Hello. Do I know you?"

She looked as if she'd been crying and when she saw me, a fresh set of tears started to well up in her eyes. It was then that I noticed it.

I was staring back into eyes that looked like my own.

"Are you my—" The words died on my lips.

When she slowly nodded, that was all I could take. Realization hit me at one hundred miles per hour, and I couldn't believe what was standing right in front of me.

My birth mother was here. Standing just outside my door.

"C-can I give you a hug?"

Her question broke through all of the thoughts swirling around my head. Those words were all it took to make the dam break. My lip began to tremble as I stared at the woman before me.

"Yes, of course."

When she opened her arms, I rushed into them full on sobbing. I'd waited for this day for so long and for it to finally be here was more than my emotions could handle.

"My baby. My beautiful baby," I heard her mumble. I don't know if she knew that I'd heard her, but it didn't matter. It was easy to see that she, too, had waited for this for so long.

When we pulled apart, we took a quick breather before she pulled me back into her arms. It was as if one hug wasn't enough, and I understood that sentiment wholeheartedly.

This time when we took a step back from one another, Ace walked over with tissues in hand and handed some to me and some to my mother. I tried my best to save my makeup, but I knew it was a disaster. There was nothing rescuing my face.

My mother spoke first. "We have so much to catch up on, and I want to know everything about you. Well, whatever you're willing to share."

"Of course. And I want to know you. Like really get to know you. Do you live here?"

She shook her head. "I live in North Dakota, and it's a long story about how that happened that I'm happy to share with you. Ace flew all the way out to meet me. He told me that he was your partner and asked if I wanted to fly to New York City to meet you. It all sounded crazy, but when he showed me a picture of you, I knew you were my baby. He even told me they kept the name I gave you. Harlow."

I never knew that my birth mother had been the one to give me my name. It always meant a lot to me because, for parts of my life, it was all I had. The added history was enough to cause me to cry again.

My birth mother tried to wipe the tears that were falling from her face, but there were too many to catch. "There's so much that I want to tell you. About why I had to give you up; I didn't want to, but all of that can come with time and as much as you're comfortable with. I'm just happy to have this opportunity to spend time with you."

"I would love that so much."

I leaned in to give Ace a hug. I whispered in his ear, "Thank you."

It finally felt as if there were no doubts that I belonged in this life.

BONUS EPILOGUE
ONE YEAR LATER

I folded my legs underneath me as I readjusted my body into a more comfortable position. I was sitting in the library at our home upstate. After a day of running errands, it felt lovely to come home and relax in front of the fireplace with a book in hand. It was often where I would find myself waiting for Ace when he was away from home and would be returning before bedtime and I'd done everything I needed to do for the day.

A couple of hours ago, I'd gone to lunch with my birth mother and had a lovely time. Over the course of the last year, we'd built a relationship with one another. I'd learned so much about her including her parents' disapproval largely influenced her decision in giving me up because she was a pregnant teen and not married. Eventually Ace offered to move her to New York State so that we could be closer to one another. She accepted and had just moved here a couple of weeks ago.

Getting back to driving myself had been a challenge I had been anticipating, but the more often I did it, the better my anxiety about it became. I was grateful to have the most patient people around me as I continued to navigate life after the accident.

Things were interesting but quiet after the deaths of Falcone and Jerald Bolton. The stress from them had lessened over time, and while it took some time, it felt good not having to live my life looking over my shoulder because of the fear that someone was trying to kill me.

When I heard the front door open, I bit my lip in an attempt to fight my grin. I couldn't wait to tell Ace about my day and to hear about his.

When he walked into the room, I couldn't help but smile. I placed my book on the cushion next to me and stood up to greet him. I pulled him into a hug and it lasted for only a moment before he dropped to one knee. He opened what appeared to be a book. Inside was a beautiful diamond ring. I don't think I'd ever seen a ring more beautiful.

"I can't wait anymore to ask you. You are the love of my life and I don't know where I would be without you. Harlow, will you marry me?"

My eyes darted between him being on his knee and the ring he was holding in this book. Finally, I stared into his eyes as tears welled up mine. I tried to find the simple word that would release the tension that had clearly built up because I hadn't responded to his question.

I found my head nodding before I was able to whisper the word we both wanted to hear. "Yes."

Happy tears fell from my eyes as I looked into his. I was ecstatic to share this moment with him; it was something we'd been talking more and more about over the last few months, but I hadn't thought about when this day would actually come.

When he slid the ring onto my finger, I couldn't take my eyes off it. I watched as my diamond ring caught the light, causing it to twinkle slightly. I couldn't help but smile at it. Happiness coursed through my mind as I stared at it.

"Did you really cut out parts of this book to propose?"

Ace chuckled. "So, you'd be pissed off at me? No. Had the box specially made for this occasion."

"Smart man."

I'd stopped believing in fairy tales long ago because they never came true. But now I was living in one.

I had a man who loved me more than anything else in the world. We had been through hell together and made it to the other side, mostly unscathed. The baggage each of us carried, separate and together, was what made us into the people we were today. While it would be easy to wish to be able to change the hardships we'd face, I wouldn't anymore.

"I love you so much," he said to me as he tucked a piece of my hair behind my ear.

"And I love you."

~

THANK you for reading The Billionaire's Vengeance! Although Harlow and Ace's story completes the Ruthless Billionaire Trilogy, you will see them and members of the Cross family in my new stories, Merciless Deception and Devious Game. Keep reading to find a sneak peek of them!

. . .

DON'T WANT to let Ace and Harlow go just yet? Click HERE to grab a bonus scene featuring the couple!

WANT to join discussions about the Ruthless Billionaire Trilogy? Click HERE to join my Reader Group on Facebook.

PLEASE JOIN my newsletter to find out the latest about the Ruthless Billionaire Trilogy and my other books!

MERCILESS DECEPTION BLURB

What we had should never have happened.

He was supposed to be just a job.

Something I'd been forced into doing because I was being blackmailed.

What I didn't expect was for it to turn into a torrid affair.

Where he fell for me,

And I for him.

Once I'd succeeded in my endeavor, I vanished.

Now he's back in my life, richer and more powerful than ever.

And he was ready to get revenge after being wronged by me.

SNEAK PEEK OF MERCILESS DECEPTION

LARA

I wanted to be anywhere but here. However, not all wishes came true. And the ones that didn't, you were often left to suffer the consequences, whether you committed the crime or not.

That was why I was here. At a gala that I had no interest in, gathering intel for something I couldn't give two shits about.

I glanced down at my wrist and checked the time. I still had a couple of hours to go before I could leave this place. With a heavy sigh, I grabbed the drink that I'd just had poured for me and brought it to my lips. At least this might help pass the time I needed to stay here go by faster. Or so I thought when my eyes landed on something across the room.

There was no way I'd just seen what I thought I saw. I blinked once and then twice, but nothing removed the image that stood before me other than closing my eyes and wishing it away.

Fuck. Why is he here tonight?

Out of all the places he could be tonight, why was he here?

Thankfully he hadn't seen me, so maybe it wouldn't be too difficult to get out of here before he noticed.

I shouldn't have come here tonight.

I was a dumbass for not listening to my gut and now I potentially had to deal with the consequences unless I could figure out another way to get out of here.

When I looked back in the direction I'd last seen him, he was gone.

Maybe this will be easier than I thought.

I grabbed my purse off the high table and slid off the chair as quickly as I could without ruining my dress. The exit was just across the room. There was a chance that I could make it there easily without being spotted, but fear of the unknown was there. I didn't know where he'd gone, and there was a chance that he was standing in the wings, waiting for me to make my next move. But I couldn't dwell on that. I needed to get out of here now because this might be the only chance I had.

I was within a few feet of the exit when someone grabbed my arm and pulled me off into a corner. I didn't bother screaming because it would have been useless here. In the circles we both ran in, no one would have bothered to help me anyway.

"Good evening, kitten."

"Parker, you lost the privilege of calling me that long ago."

"Says who? You?" His dark chuckle sounded anything but joyous. He stormed toward me with a look in his eye that was frightening. "I don't take instructions from anyone and you should know that by now."

I did know that. I'd seen him in action, in and out of the bedroom, and that proved just that.

"What are you doing here?"

There was no chance in hell I was telling him that. "None of your business."

"But it is my business. Now say it." His grip tightened on my arm, but not enough to make me wince. He knew what he was doing.

"I'm here to meet someone."

"Who? Or is it the same scam you tried to run on me several years ago?"

I refused to confirm or deny his suspicions even if he was wrong. Dead wrong.

"I've thought about you a lot over the years."

I hadn't expected him to continue talking, let alone say that. Nor had I expected his words to freeze me in place.

"Our time together was cut short, but maybe this was fate."

My head jerked back. "What the hell are you talking about?"

"You know exactly what I'm talking about."

I did but refused to admit it. I pushed my shoulders back and looked him directly in his eyes. "What we had is long gone. I've moved on, and you should too. Now, let. Go. Of. Me."

His eyes studied me coolly, removing any ounce of confidence I had. And he still hadn't let go of my arm.

Instead of asking him again, I snatched my arm out of his grasp and took a step back, putting some much-needed distance between the two of us.

"Leave me alone. It's better for both of us this way."

I took two steps backward before turning on my heel and walking away as quickly as I could in these sky-high heels I had on. He wasn't supposed to be here, but he was. Now I had to deal with the consequences.

While he hadn't said a word after I turned away, his body language told me all I needed to know. The look in his eyes told me that he would do anything but stay away.

Merciless Deception is available for pre-order and will be released in 2023.

DEVIOUS GAME BLURB

I left Brentson in the dead of night and made a promise that I would never return.

I was determined to leave my past behind, but here's the thing about it:

It always has a way of hunting you down.

Now, I'm face-to-face with Nash Henson, my ex-boyfriend, heir to the Henson fortune, and crowned king of Brentson University.

He'll never forgive me for what I've done.

And when he's done playing his game with me, there won't be anything left.

Because he's determined to destroy me.

SNEAK PEEK OF DEVIOUS GAME

My hand tightened on the steering wheel as I drove past a familiar sign.

Welcome to Brentson

The elaborate sign was meant to offer a warm embrace and show Brentson's hospitality. Except I felt anything but welcomed.

The only thing keeping me calm was the cool breeze that felt like a gentle whisper on my face as I drove through Brentson. Late August into early September was always one of my favorite times in the town. With the leaves already starting to change, it painted a pretty picture of my home-town. What should have been a time to bask in remembering the good times I spent here was anything but. I spent many afternoons during high school at Smith's Ice Cream Parlor—still standing and as popular as ever. Many of my memories there included Nash Henson, someone I tried to forget over the years. And I failed every single time.

A few minutes later, and with a heavy sigh, I steered my old Toyota Camry onto Brentson University's campus. Another welcome sign beaconed me home. Butterflies collided in my stomach as I took in my surroundings. What once had been my dream school was now my living nightmare. As a kid, I'd hoped that I would one day enroll at BU. Now that I had the opportunity, it felt as if hell had swallowed me whole.

Transferring to Brentson had been a lot simpler than I thought it would be, and for that I was grateful. Not having to deal with that on top of everything else was crucial in helping me prepare for this move across the country.

I looked at the map on my phone before turning off the GPS. I knew where I was now. Some things had changed in the last three years, but most of what I remembered about this town had stayed the same. Recalling the last couple of directions from the GPS, I navigated to a small home and pulled into the driveway. It looked well maintained, which wasn't surprising given that it was owned by the university.

Before I had an opportunity to move, the front door swung open and out popped a petite woman with a huge smile on her face.

"You're here!"

I nodded and gave her a small smile through the windshield. Seeing Izzy Deacon did nothing to calm the nerves building in my body. With a shaky hand, I stepped out of the car, locked up, and took a deep breath. She bounded down the stairs and pulled me into her arms.

It felt wonderful to be reunited with Izzy again. We had seen each other in person a couple of times over the years, but it had been months since we last hung out.

"Glad you made it here okay. I've been dying to hear more about why you decided to transfer here for our senior year."

There was only so much I could tell her because I needed to do my best to make sure that no one else would be affected by this mess. "Izzy, I'll fill you in. I promise."

That seemed to satisfy her as a smile reappeared on her face.

"We have to get you settled. You mentioned that you were having trouble finding a place and I wanted you to know that you could always stay with me. I know there is no way in hell you'd go back home."

"I appreciate the offer, but I know I'll find something near campus."

Izzy crossed her arms in a huff. "Well, you should stay with me until you do."

I shifted my weight from one foot to the other. "Okay."

"Yay!" Izzy exclaimed with childlike glee. "It's been way too long since we've spent time together. I've been waiting for this ever since you said you were coming back." Without another word, Izzy pulled me into another hug.

"I've been looking forward to this, too." That wasn't a lie. I had looked forward to spending time with Izzy since I knew I was coming back to Brentson.

"Oh, no."

Izzy whispered this in my ear because we were still hugging. It was clear that something was wrong. When her arms loosened, and I regained the ability to move, I looked over my shoulder before doing a one-eighty. Standing across the street was the last person I was ready to see again.

My breath caught in my chest when his eyes landed on me.

Nash.

He still looked as handsome as I remembered. Any hope I had that he might have forgotten all the things I did was dashed when his eyes narrowed. And he glared at me. If he could have snarled at me from where he was, he would have. He wasn't alone, and soon the guy with him drew his attention away from me. But, as he left, he gave me one final stare.

I watched him walk away, not blaming him one bit for his reaction.

My name might be Raven Goodwin, but I was far from good.

Devious Game is available for pre-order and will be released in summer 2022.

ABOUT THE AUTHOR

Bri loves a good romance, especially ones that involve a hot anti-hero. That is why she likes to turn the dial up a notch with her own writing. Her Broken Cross series is her debut dark romance series.

She spends most of her time hanging out with her family, plotting her next novel, or reading books by other romance authors.

briblackwood.com

ALSO BY BRI BLACKWOOD